Praise for *Affection: an m...*

Shortlisted, Queensland Premier's Award for non-fiction ...0
Shortlisted, Biography of the Year,
Australian Book Industry Awards 2010

'Sexy and beautifully written. *Affection* is a moving portrait
and an absorbing read...An unforgettable book.' James Frey

'To focus on the prurient aspects of this memoir...is to
miss its gorgeous heart...*Affection* is lushly written, a vivid
and unabashed account of a woman coming to terms
with her body.' *Courier-Mail*

'A rare feat...Beneath the surface sexuality, *Affection*'s
triumph is that of an assured novelist of any genre. She sets
a scene in curt but vivid detail and injects emotional
vibrancy into even cursory encounters.' *Sunday Age*

'A lyrical gem. Kneen has a rare gift for constructing the
most exquisite architectures of narrative and meaning from
simple and elegant prose. Sometimes confronting, sometimes
hilarious, and always amazingly honest.' John Birmingham

'Astonishing...Powerfully and voyeuristically erotic,
a relentless yet tender examination of the body's relationship
to self-worth...An extraordinary debut.' Matthew Condon

'Beautifully written, painfully honest...Kneen's stark,
sensuous writing style and clear-eyed honesty are
immensely appealing.' *Big Issue*

'Sex in *Affection* is well written, but it's the contemplation in between that really shines. Insightful, evocative and bluntly, but never gratuitously, honest…Sexy, sad and deeply satisfying.' Emily Maguire, *Age*

'*Affection* is that rare beast; a sexual memoir that is not only uniquely interesting and daringly explicit but is also poetic, offbeat, confronting and funny.'
Linda Jaivin, *Australian*

Praise for *Triptych*

'I have great admiration for this book and frankly enjoyed reading it.' *Sydney Morning Herald*

'This is an astounding look at different sorts of love and Kneen is, above all, a sensualist.' *Adelaide Advertiser*

'With nods to Anaïs Nin and Vladimir Nabokov, Kneen writes with tenderness, joy and delight…
Delightful, courageous and juicy.' *Big Issue*

Krissy Kneen is best known as a writer of literary erotica (*Triptych*) and sexual memoir (*Affection*). *Steeplechase* is her first novel and her first non-erotic work. She lives in Brisbane with her husband.
furiousvaginas.com
twitter.com/krissykneen

KRISSY KNEEN
STEEPLECHASE

TEXT PUBLISHING MELBOURNE AUSTRALIA

textpublishing.com.au

The Text Publishing Company
Swann House
22 William Street
Melbourne Victoria 3000
Australia

First published by The Text Publishing Company, 2013

Cover design by WH Chong
Page design by Imogen Stubbs

Printed in Australia by Griffin Press an Accredited ISO AS/NZS 14001:2004 Environmental Management System printer.

National Library of Australia Cataloguing-in-Publication entry:
Author: Kneen, Krissy, 1968–
Title: Steeplechase / by Krissy Kneen.
ISBN: 9781922079879 (pbk.)
ISBN: 9781922148100 (eBook)
Dewey Number: A823.4

This book is printed on paper certified against the Forest Stewardship Council® Standards. Griffin Press holds FSC chain-of-custody certification SGS-COC-005088. FSC promotes environmentally responsible, socially beneficial and economically viable management of the world's forests.

For Chris Somerville

'I leaf again and again through these miserable memories, and keep asking myself, was it then, in the glitter of that remote summer, that the rift in my life began; or was my excessive desire for that child only the first evidence of an inherent singularity?'

VLADIMIR NABOKOV, *Lolita*

Prologue

My sister Emily likes ponies and show jumping and arenas. Sometimes I jump with her because she wants me to. I throw my head back and make the horse's sound but it is never the right sound. She corrects me with her perfect whinnying, her neck exposed, her knees kicking high, a canter. I am not a good horse. I have not studied them as she has, chapter books where the beasts gallop, picture books thick with taut flanks and staring eyes. I jump over the obstacles that she sets for me but I never get a ribbon for my effort. Sometimes she whips me with a hickory stick which is not made of hickory at all, but instead a branch fallen from the ghost gum in the corner of the yard. She tells me that I am a bad horse, a lazy horse, a slow horse, and I take the whipping silently because it is true. I am a bad horse. I am not any kind of horse at all.

The steeplechase is dangerous. She outlines the difficulties with her serious face, her furrowed brow. Horses fall, she tells me, riders die. She says that sometimes, on a difficult hurdle, a jockey will fall. The horse will be landing, its feet chopping the soil into clumps and if the rider falls into the path of the hooves his head will split.

'It happens too quickly,' she tells me. 'The cameras are all watching the jump and then the hoof clomps down onto the rider's head and the brains come out and it is too quick for the television crew to cut the filming.'

'They could cut it afterwards, before it goes on TV.'

'They film it live. The steeplechase is always live. But they don't replay the jump in slow motion if the rider has been trampled to death. This is out of respect for the family.'

I am sceptical but she is older and her description of a particular death seems real enough. She describes the way the man flips up and over the front of the horse. Too quick for him to scream or even show surprise. The hoof thumps down on his skull and his head snaps open like a grape when you press it between two fingers. The brain comes out and it is like grey pudding splattering up out of a dropped bowl. The other hooves tramp down onto the rider's chest and legs and stomach and the horse falls forward, bending at its knees, its chin sliding across the choppy turf.

'They shoot the horse in the head.' She leans in conspiratorially to tell me this, her eyes wide, her breath laced with a forbidden sweetness from the Redskin she stole from the shop when our grandmother wasn't looking. I can see the traces of the candy like lipstick on her mouth and for an awful second I imagine her taking my head between her hands and kissing me firmly on the lips.

'That is the tragedy.' She leans back and grins, all blood-red teeth. 'They shoot the horse. It was never the horse's fault to begin with, but they shoot it in the head, on camera, and there is no difference between the brains of a horse and the brains of a man. I've seen it. So I know.'

She has set the hurdles to reflect a great degree of difficulty. Some of them are too high. One is perched over what she calls a ditch, the edge of a garden bed with flowers spread below it. One is a sand trap, one is a leap through the arms of the swing. Two of them are too close, only a single galloping step between them. We walk the course, which is apparently what they do in real steeple-chases, bringing the horse's nose to touch each hedge and ditch and creek. She mimes her horse, pulling the reins and gently patting the air where its nose would be. Sometimes she makes the horse's noises, huffing and sniffing, getting the scent of the course that it will soon tackle.

I have no such invisible horse. As I walk the course I imagine my own legs snapping as I trip over the swing set, falling into the pit of marigolds. When we are back at the starting line she has stepped into her horse. Her legs are high kicking. She sidles forward, back, kicks at the ground. I imagine that it will be my fall that is televised, and my sister's hooves, shod in her black sensible shoes, that will be stamping on my head, popping my skull like a grape.

'Riders, mount your stallions.'

They are always stallions. My sister rides a black one or perhaps inhabits is a better word for what is happening beside me, head lowered, pawing the thirsty yellow lawn, she snorts and stamps and grunts. More like a pig than a horse it seems, but I do not say so.

3

'Ready, mark, go.'

We are off. I run towards the first hurdle, a chair upended. I have to jump far enough to miss the back of it, which is lying flat on the ground. I run and leap and I have passed the first test but I am already a good three metres behind.

I want to play her games. I want to love horses with the same uncomplicated passion. I try to mimic her drawings, but my horse's legs are never sturdy enough, the knees seem to bend at the wrong angle. My horse always looks as if it is broken, fallen from her steeplechase and waiting on the page for the bullet in the head. I clear the second jump and the third, but the leap through the swing seems quite impossible, even as I watch my sister grab the chains and swing herself up and through, pulling her knees up tight against her chest. I stop at the base of the swing and step through, one heavy foot after the other. And this is the end of the race for me. I bypass the marigold trap and climb over the ladder instead of jumping it.

She stands panting at the finish line and she is still a horse, sweating, nostrils flared, eyes wider than a human gaze. And as she watches me, walking, bypassing the last few hurdles, there is all the animal derision she can muster in that flat stare. I am not good enough. I am not fast enough. I am a slow, ugly disappointment. Horse becomes rider as she turns and flicks her ponytail in my direction, and steps gracefully in her jodhpurs towards home.

PART ONE

23 Years Later My Sister Calls

I am recovering from an operation when my sister calls. The drugs they have given me are morphine based. They make my skin itch. I wake from painless sleep and sort back through dreams that plunge me into moments in my life I had forgotten. I woke up in the hospital. After the operation. Perhaps still in the theatre. All I knew was that it was bright and I was in pain and if I didn't stand up and stretch out I would die from it. Then I was asleep again, and when I opened my eyes they asked me about the pain.

I felt removed from it. Even now it is painful but it does not hurt. It is at arm's length, although I can't seem to bend at the waist or cough without feeling all my muscles tense, as if I am protecting myself from some injury that my flesh has forgotten. I suppose it hurts somewhere beyond the morphine. My body is growing a shell and all the cut-into, prodded-at, torn-out places are quivering inside that shell.

I wake at home, in my own bed, and I am lonely and tired and I am hungry but not hungry as well, and strangely craving the kind of sour, hard candy that I don't particularly like. I think perhaps I am overwhelmingly sad and want someone to take care of me. I think about my family for the first time in a long time. How I would hate for my grandmother to be here now, hovering over me, protecting me from every stray draught. But. Despite that, I would love some of her homemade soup and bread fresh from the oven and the comfort of her ridiculous proverbs and senseless wisdoms. I am thinking about my family when the phone rings.

Maybe I am too sad to pick up the phone. I can feel my own tears welling, held back with great effort as you might hold back vomit. I am curled in a corner of the lounge and the phone is ringing and ringing. I have placed the two phones within reach, the home phone and my mobile. Standing is too difficult. I take a breath and pick up both phones and realise that it is my mobile, the weight of it buzzing in the palm of my hand. I flip it open and answer, mouth full of sleep, lazy tongue struggling for a greeting.

'Hello?'

And then my own voice, echoed back to me. 'Hello? Hello?' There is a slight delay, which adds to the strangeness of the moment. My first thought is that I am talking to myself on the phone. It has been years since my last visit to the psychiatrist. I am no longer mad. I am cured, and yet this sudden odd displacement of self drops me back into all the old worries.

I press the phone to my ear and listen. My own voice on the phone. Me, somewhere else, talking to myself, slightly delayed. I imagine for a moment that I will have something profound to say to myself. Bec, I will say, I am about to tell you the exact moment of your death.

'Who is this?' I ask myself, only it is not me, of course. Even before she speaks I can feel the realisation washing over me, a cold wave and all my blood running away with it.

'Emily,' she says. 'Your sister.'

'I'm on morphine,' I tell her. I should feel relieved. I am not falling back into madness. This is not another Bec on the phone, this is Emily. My sister. My sister who I have not spoken to for over twenty years.

'I heard you had an operation,' she says. 'You had your gall-bladder out.'

'Yeah.' And then I wonder how she knew this. Maybe she called work. I should ask her.

I am going to ask her but she says, 'So you're okay?'

'Yeah.' But how would she know where I work? All of these impossibilities making my mouth taste dry and a little bitter on the back of my palate.

'Well I just thought I would call.'

'Thanks.'

I hold the phone to my ear and it seems there is no blood in my body. I am cold and I am sure I am paler than I was before the phone rang. I feel nothing, the pain is distant, but my body has shut down, conserving its energy. This is a fight or flight response, I read this somewhere, some popular science column in a magazine, all the useless facts we learned in home-school chiming discordantly in my head all these years later.

So then, fight or flight. I feel a calm readiness and if I am forced to flee I will flee with every scrap of energy I have stockpiled, my limbs pounding, my wounded body hurtling at breakneck speed.

'Okay, as long as you're doing well.'

'I am.'

'Well I bought you a ticket to Beijing. In case you want to come over.'

'Oh.'

'Cause we talked about going overseas together. I know we talked about Paris and Berlin but I'm in Beijing so maybe…'

'Oh,' I say. And, 'When? Why are you in Beijing?'

'I booked your ticket for your birthday. A week before your birthday. That's enough time to get holidays? You have work, right?'

'Yes, at uni. But that's not much time.'

'But enough time to get a replacement or something?'

'Maybe. I don't—Beijing?'

'Yeah. In China.'

'You bought me a ticket already? Without asking me first?'

'Yeah.'

'Do I have to say yes or no now?'

'No. You can call me. When the morphine wears off.'

'I don't have your number.'

'Well you do now because this is a mobile, right?'

'Oh. I suppose.' And then the wave of sadness is back and I can barely speak from it.

'I'll go then.'

And I want to say wait but my throat is locked up so I just nod, uselessly, the phone clutched too tight against my head and heating up my ear, probably giving me cancer.

'Bye Bec.'

'Bye Emily.'

And in the silence when the connection is severed I wonder

if she noticed how similar our voices still are. If she was also taken aback by the identical inflections. That accent that is just a little too formal, the accent that marks us as children of immigrants, that edge of an Australian twang that we practised together as children, mimicking the kids in town till we thought we had it just right. That shared longing to fit in when it was inevitable that we never would.

I am still holding the phone and my ear is still hot and my body is still cold, and I force myself to take the phone away from my head and search its memory for the last incoming call. I store the number under one word, 'sister'. I should have used her name but it is all I can think of in this moment. Sister. My sister. My sister just called me and I spoke to her. I imagine the words as if they were written in a book: *twenty-three years later my sister called.* I flip the phone closed, then open. Check through my address book just to see that her number is still there. Check the recent calls and it is true. She called me. Last incoming call. *Sister.* My sister.

I hold the phone against my chest and give in to the insistent tug of the morphine. I taste my grandmother's soup on my tongue and I might be fifteen again. I might be ill and recovering on the couch. I might be listening to the sound of my grandmother locking the doors and windows, that rhythmic slapping of drawn bolts, locks slipping into place, windows sliding on their rail. Before it all came apart, before the terrible thing. I close my eyes and I am transported to a time when I felt safe and secure and locked up tight.

Locked Tight

She locks all the doors and all the windows. I hear the rattle of keys taken from a hook by the door. It is summer and the air is stale and damp in the house. Perhaps outside there is some small breeze, something with an edge of cool to cut through all this heat and sweat, but our grandmother begins her rounds and there will be no evening relief.

We listen to the rattle and scrape as one window after another is pulled to. The jangle of keys, each window a different key and she must find it on the ring and then turn it in the lock before moving on. The house is a box for warm bodies. The collective heat of us accumulates.

I sit up in bed when our Oma comes in, but Emily does not stir. She is reading, turned onto her side, propped up with two white pillows. I hear the lazy *shick* of her page turning but apart from this she remains very still.

My grandmother is a short nugget of a woman, all wire and muscle. There is no stillness in her. There is a fat metal bar on her key ring. This is a weapon. If she is attacked she will use it, a heavy blow to the head. I believe she could overpower anyone.

She rarely talks about the past but there is this one story. She was sent away for safety, hoisted up onto a train. She was only young, our age or even younger, and she didn't have a proper ticket. When the guard came he tried to make her leave her seat but she hooked her fingers around the arms of her chair and held on. Eventually he shrugged and moved off, hoping to find an easier offender in another carriage. My grandmother has always been fearless. 'I stay alive,' she says in her thick guttural accent. Her fearlessness has saved her many times, I suspect. I wonder about all the other times, the ones that she has not named. I watch her sinewy arms reaching and pulling and locking and it is impossible not to compare myself to her. I am more like my mother, round and squat and puffy in the cheeks.

She locks the window and turns in the doorway to face us: my bed and my sister's. She is standing on the line that runs the length of the room as if here at the exact place that divides Emily's half from mine she might speak to both of us and prove she is not playing favourites, which is something that she simply refuses to do.

'Don't stay up ruining your eyes.'

I nod, but Emily says nothing. She flicks a page. Our grandmother pulls the door closed behind her and Emily rolls onto her back and holds the book open over her face. Her shoulders shake slightly. Maybe she is crying or maybe she is laughing. It is impossible to know what Emily is feeling at any moment. One emotion seems to morph so quickly into another. I hear our grandmother moving down the corridor and into our mother's room. Emily said once that she remembered our mother as she was before. She said she looked like a princess, but it seems impossible now.

There are thirteen windows in our house if you include the sliding glass doors. There are two heavy wooden doors. I count them, the soft squeal of my mother's window, the twin snappings of the windows in the studio. Our grandmother locks the windows to protect us, this is what she says. There are people outside, murderers, rapists, bad people who would hurt the children. She has been put in charge of the care of the children. Our mother has faltered in this task and it has fallen to our grandmother. We are her first concern, apparently.

Sometimes, like tonight, I hear her pause in her locking routine. She stands in her studio and I know she is looking at the art. She is the guardian of paintings worth more than all the land in this town. Work by famous artists is placed in her temporary care while she picks at the dirt and sludge of years, stripping everything back to its original glory. Sometimes she lets us come into her studio with our hands behind our backs to look. There will be some new work there, propped up on an easel or flat on the table, and it will be just another painting, some rich lady in pearls, some man at his desk, some landscape with trees, perhaps a lake.

I settle down onto the pillow and look towards my sister's side of the room, the calm side, the neatness butting up against my chaos. My sister is painting another horse. She rarely paints anything else. A huge majestic animal, chest heaving, eye turned to face the world, large and somehow seeming angry and frightened at the same time. It seems incongruous, this wild creature leaping from a canvas in the midst of the order that is my sister's side of the room.

'Old people die of heatstroke.'

'What?' I am whispering. Our grandmother is still just across the hallway, distracted by something in her study, picking at spots of glaze with a toothpick or easing dust away with a soft, dry brush.

'Old people are so afraid they lock all the doors and windows and then they get heatstroke and they die, or else there is some kind of electrical fault but they are deadbolted inside and the fire burns them to death.'

'Okay,' I say. 'I didn't know that.'

'Don't you defend her.'

She is speaking too loudly. I would like to tell Emily that I am not defending her but Oma would hear me say this. I bite on my bottom lip and roll over, away from the clean side of the room, my sister's side. I look towards the stuff I have left in uneasy piles leaning against a wall splattered with blobs of paint and coloured fingerprints.

Our grandmother turns the light out in her studio and continues on her rounds, the windows in the kitchen, the windows in the lounge room, the back door with its bolt and lock. We are safe now, the night will pass without a home invasion. Safe, protected, locked up tight.

Life Drawing

I pause outside the room. I am a little late. There is a rustling inside, wild creatures pacing in their cage. I know how lion tamers must feel, the effort it takes to perform the confidence trick. I set my face to smiling. I have put some effort into my clothing, just formal enough, just a little bit casual and the socks are mismatched, which was not planned but which is good for the look nonetheless. I am self-conscious. I am self-conscious about my own self-consciousness.

As I open the door the rustling abates and they are all there waiting. The girls are too thin and fashionably shy. They wear little cardigans and cute red shoes with buckles. Their hair is braided or cut into a fringe or tugged into pigtails. The boys are elegantly crumpled. They have almost all mastered the art of boredom. They sit on their own, preened and perfect and so uber-cool that even a simple conversation must be a carefully thought out interplay of style and ideas. The room smells of linseed oil and even here it is a scent that transports me back to childhood.

The easels are scattered about the edges of the room. The students hover close to but not directly in front of their sketchpads so as not to seem too keen. The model is young, quite pretty. She is wearing a simple wrap-around dress and under this she will not be wearing underwear. Lately they have all been beautiful. This one has a glow of bright red hair and perfect cheekbones. Her eyes are wide and intelligent.

He is talking with her. He is always talking with someone when I arrive. He is the only person in the room with no self-awareness. This is how he disarms me. His shoes are old and there is tape on one, holding the sole on. His jumper is faded, but not in that funky op-shop old-made-new way. It is just an old jumper with a stain over his heart where a pen has leaked. His hair is a sweaty mess. He is plumper than the other boys and his skin has a sheen to it that makes me think he was out last night, drinking.

The model grins at him, her face lighting up with pleasure. She laughs. He likes to make girls laugh. Sometimes he makes me laugh too.

I ease my satchel down and stand at the front of the room. There is a desk here, and a whiteboard that is never used. I perch on the desk and slowly, one by one, the pretty, bored faces turn in my direction. There is a dull ache in my stomach. It feels like I have been hollowed out, which is fair enough. I suppose I have been.

'So we meet again.' There are some nods, a few grins. John whispers something to the model and she giggles prettily before standing, tugging her clothes tighter around her as if she is reluctant to shed them at all.

She smiles at me. Very attractive. I may have seen her before. Or not, six hundred models a year and all the drawings the same. The pose with the head bent forward, the one leaning back like a dancer, the lying on the floor as if dead or sleeping. There are only so many poses a body can adopt. She unties her dress and unwraps herself. Some of them like to do this in another room. Either way, they end up naked. The students are used to this now but there is still a certain awkwardness. There is never any inter-action between student and model, except John of course. I watch him lowering his easel to chair height, the canvas is unbalanced and he grabs at it noisily. The girl closest to him smiles and they exchange raised eyebrows. John holds his finger to his lips and her smile becomes a wide grin. He is charming in his awkwardness.

'So,' I tell them. 'You know the drill, five-second poses, then thirty-second poses, then some longer ones. You okay with that?' This to the model. She has a name. It is on the job sheet that I have buried somewhere in my notes. When I started working here I used to make a point of remembering their names. Now I just stand and take my watch off my wrist and hold it, mostly for show. 'Start,' I say, and then, 'Change.

'Change.

'Change.'

The model lunges into impossible shapes. Perhaps she is a dancer or a gymnast, her breasts never seem to sag. She is gor-geous. 'Change, change, change.'

Little stick drawings, lines really, just the general shape and movement. They are no better or worse than any other students I have had. I walk slowly around the circle of easels and the works are interchangeable. Sharp quick lines of varying thickness. Some more interested in the curve of the back, some of them breast-men and women, drawing the pretty pert hang, the ever-changing direction of the nipple. Some of them concentrate on the hair.

John has never been good at the quick drawing. I walk behind him and notice that today he has decided not to draw the model at all. Instead he has begun to sketch my desk, the model's dress hanging from it like a dead pelt, the puddle of skirt lapping at the ground beneath. Nothing quick about this drawing, he has started with shadow and is drawing back to the highlights. This is something my sister used to do. I recognise the intensity of the strokes.

'Okay. A longer one now. Say, twenty minutes?' The model nods. I walk, slowly, glancing. I do not interfere. I am here if they want me but they never do, these bright young things with their fifties dresses and their mad hair. When I walk past John's easel, I see that he has begun to draw the model, finally. A close study of her face, politely ignoring her nakedness.

My guts feel empty. An organ has been taken out of my body and it feels like my flesh is rearranging to accommodate it. I walk from easel to easel with this empty space inside me. I wonder if I came back to work too soon.

John glances up as I walk by his easel and he is all grin. He wants me to like his work. And I do, but his need for my approval is even more charming. It is an effort for me not to rest a com-forting hand on his shoulder. Instead I nod, and smile back a little and he goes back to his drawing with more enthusiasm. The woman in the picture looks pretty but sad. I do not see this in the model. This is something he has added, this edge of melancholy.

When I complete the circuit and begin another slow pass of the easels I notice that he has begun to draw one of her breasts and I feel a sudden, inexplicable stab of jealousy. I should be at home on the couch with my pretentious subtitled DVDs and my Nabokov and framed Gentileschi prints.

John looked through my video collection when he came over that first time and he laughed and asked me where the comedies were. *I don't like comedy* seemed like a bad answer at the time and it is still a terrible excuse. I am like the rest of my students—a cliché. I wear my op-shop treasures and never watch television and frown at anything that is supposed to make me laugh. John makes me laugh.

I frown at John now because he has moved down to the genitals and instead of making them half-there like the other students do, he has drawn in every fold and line and the model now looks more than naked. She looks exposed. I look past his cartridge block to where she is lying and yes, her legs are just that tiny bit parted and from this angle one of her labia is larger than the other and protruding slightly, but none of the other students have reproduced it in quite this detail. In John's eyes, we have an incredibly well realised face, one breast, a vulva. He finishes it with the neatly trimmed pubic hair and moves down to the feet. He starts to detail the toes one at a time and I move on to the other students who have spent more time on the general curve of the hip, easing over the genitals with vague pencil strokes. I look at my watch. Half an hour to go.

'Okay,' I say. 'Time for one more pose.'

★

'You have three years' worth of holidays accrued. You have four years of sick days.'

I shake my head. 'I know. I know.'

Ed dresses like a teenager and he really shouldn't. His runners are too bright. His T-shirt is ripped and the hair on his back shows through it. Sometimes, but thankfully not today, he wears a skinny tie over the top of his T-shirt.

'I thought I'd be fine the next day. Keyhole sounds like something really small, you know?'

'You've had a part of your body removed.'

'Yeah,' I say, 'and they wouldn't let me keep it, not even the stones.'

'What? That's crazy, that is your body. That belongs to you. I know someone who was offered his amputated leg to take home.'

'Yeah, go figure.'

'How do they expect us to make art? What, do they tell Damian Hirst he isn't allowed to take his appendix home?'

I have reached my office door and I stand there with my fingers resting on the handle and he hovers. He is an odd man, awkward, but his miniatures are great and the students are fond of him. He grins and I am reminded that I am fond of him too.

He puts his hand on my shoulder and gives me his serious face, which is actually quite amusing so I smile. 'Just take tomorrow off. For me. And book in holidays. A week, two weeks, four months. Take the rest of the year off. Go hire a studio and do some work. This isn't a private university, this is the public frigging service.' He shakes his head paternally. 'There will be no burn-out on my watch.'

I look past Ed and John is there, leaning against the wall at the end of the corridor, looking anywhere but in my direction.

'I'll take tomorrow off.'

'Good,' he says. 'Great. And your holidays?'

'Yeah. I'll take some. Soon. I promise. After the exhibition.'

For a terrible moment I think he might hug me. He steps forward and makes a little awkward gesture with his hand, which might be a wave or an aborted attempt to touch my arm.

'Have a good day off,' he says. I watch him walk past the place where John is leaning against the wall, then I step into my office and close the door.

It is a room filled with paintings, postcard-sized prints and some larger ones, students' work. And then there is the wall that is devoted to my sister. Pictures of sad men with flames eating their shoulders. Happy children with only darkness where their eyes should be. A boy with blowflies swarming where there should be only laughter. I wait a moment till he knocks, softly, a cat scratching. He knows I will be waiting.

I press the palms of my hands against my eyes. If I wait long enough he might go away.

The Pecking Order

We pull up outside the shop in town and there are kids playing in the gutter. They have a ball that bounces erratically. They chase after it and laugh and fall over themselves trying to catch it. Their older brothers perch on the bench and smoke cigarettes. I can see the neck of a beer bottle jutting out of a boy's jacket. They watch us jump down out of the back of the van. There is something not right about our clothing. Their clothes are bought and ours are made. Their shirts are bright with album covers on the front, our collared shirts seem prim.

'Yokels,' Emily leans over to whisper it into my ear. I snort because it is funny, but then after a moment I realise it is not funny at all. We walk into the shop, our grandmother, our mother and us, all similarly dressed. Our mother stands at the door. Everyone knows about our mother. No matter how tight you lock the doors the truth still sneaks out in a small town. She looks okay if you don't talk to her. A little vague perhaps but she sticks close to us and keeps her head down and a stranger would never even know. It would be easier to leave her at home of course, but she might try to turn on the stove and then leave the gas on and burn the house down and the child protection would come and take us. She has to come with us when we go out but it isn't so bad. Our grandmother says that at one time she used to play with matches, so we have to be vigilant and make sure she is safe when Oma is in her study or out changing the straw for the animals.

I linger outside the shop watching the local kids. I would like to join in their game with the ball. There is something dangerous and exciting about perching on a bench, smoking a cigarette, sneaking beer. I stare at one of the boys, a skinny tall boy with his T-shirt rolled up at the sleeve and a bulge where his cigarette packet presses out of the cotton. He stares back, winks. I turn quickly and trail inside after my family.

Today we are allowed a treat. It will be a long drive. Two hours if there is no traffic. We have a basket of food, roast vegetables baked into fresh buns, a quiche cut into thick slices, herbal tea in a thermos. Emily and I can choose one of the bad things each to take with us, an ice-cream or a can of sugary drink or a chocolate bar. We must choose carefully. There will be no chance to rectify a bad decision. I have been thinking I will have a Polly Waffle because of the packet, which is pink, and because it is longer than the other chocolate bars. I know that Emily will have an ice-cream. She always picks an ice-cream and she always finishes it too quickly because it melts in the hot car and drips down her hands onto her sleeves. I will take my time with my chocolate bar, whichever one I choose, and it will last almost the whole two hours. I will leave a piece the same thickness as my thumb and I will give this to my sister because she will have spent the whole last hour watching me take excruciatingly small bites of chocolate, counting the distance between towns by the size of the bar melting in my fist.

Our hands are sticky when we clamber out from the back of the van. Our grandmother tips some water into the cups of our palms and we shake them dry over a flowerbed.

The museum is my favourite place in the world. I like it better than the art gallery, which is where we normally go so the museum is a special and unexpected pleasure. The doors slide open and it is always cold inside. It is a relief after the relentless sun on the top of the kombi. The museum smells like dust and time. It smells like history, crumbling parchment, old carpet, bones. We are greeted by the skeletal bodies of condors stretched out above us, flying in formation. Behind them there are other birds, some large, like the picked-clean bodies of pelicans, and some of them tiny, sparrows, finches, all of them wired into positions of flight, wings outstretched, angled down to catch an undetectable breeze.

Our grandmother carries a large wooden box. I know there is a painting inside but in a museum it could be anything really, bones from something extinct, a dinosaur, perhaps something deformed, the conjoined skeleton of a lamb. We trail behind her down the escalator. She is strong. The box is heavy but she carries it easily. I notice her wiry muscles. She is old but she is tough, our grandmother. *Never give up and never complain.* Past the Sepik River display, deep into the bowels of the museum, the primordial back rooms where the dark is so thick that the pinpoint shafts of light carve it like cake.

Our grandmother speaks with the man from the museum. He

is a doctor and seems important. They talk about the Cretaceous era and then about herbivores, a skeleton found somewhere in the desert and then they talk about art, more pieces that they have in their collection, most of them in storage, some of them in need of work. She needs the work, that's what she tells him and then they both look towards our mother who is sitting quiet as usual in a chair in the corner. After this they talk about money. I am not supposed to listen in to conversations about money and so I wander over to where my sister is peering into a fish tank on a bench.

The tank is surrounded by bottles filled with dead things, lizards, insects, grubs, all suspended in a yellowed liquid. The tank is empty except for some twigs and leaves and dirt, or so it seems. I shrug and put my finger to a jar with a centipede inside it, but my sister taps on the glass tank, drawing my attention. There is a slight rustling of the leaves. I lean in closer and she points. I step back suddenly. There is a cockroach inside, or at least it looks like a cockroach, but it is as big as the palm of my hand and the same colour as the leaves in the tank.

'In Burma,' my sister says, 'if you disobey the government they tie you down in a room full of these cockroaches and let them slowly eat your face.'

I don't really believe her but I step back anyway. She told me the same thing once about a giant crustacean called a coconut crab. Still, I watch the huge insect burrow under the leaf litter and it seems plausible.

'Put your hand inside the tank,' she whispers. She takes my hand and I lock my arm stiff and tight. She is stronger than I am and I watch in horror as my hand is pulled closer to the fish tank.

The doctor is standing behind us suddenly. Emily drops my hand and she is all sugar and lace as she points to the tank.

'Big bugs, huh?'

She nods.

'Natives. We breed everything larger here, don't we?'

He leads us into another room and makes us tea with real milk from a carton that isn't powdered and lumpy.

The doctor shows us another glass case that seems to be filled with more dead branches. I search the bottom for cockroaches, but Emily nods and points and when I adjust my vision I notice that some of the branches are insects that look like sticks and leaves.

There are more jars on shelves and he shows me the preserved body of a snake that has mistakenly eaten an echidna. The spines poke out through its skin.

'It is terrible what desperation drives us to,' he says, and his voice is so deep and rich he might as well be a radio presenter and not a doctor at all.

In the car on the way back our mother starts to sing, just softly, a little tuneless song that seems stuck on a loop. Our grandmother shushes her but she sticks with it. She is still singing when we pull into a little town for lunch. We sit in the park there with the last of our buns and leave Mother in the car to eat her lunch alone. If we took her with us she would only draw attention to us. Our grandmother stares at the kombi all through lunch and I suppose she is just checking up on our mother, making sure she does nothing to harm the wooden crates filled with paintings in the back of the car. Priceless, she called them. Actually this means very expensive rather than worth nothing at all.

'Your mother is very smart,' she says and I glance over my shoulder to where she is sitting, stiff-backed, staring out towards the parked van. 'When something snaps it doesn't mean you are not still smart. It is like a watch when the winding mechanism is broken, it still has the potential to tell the time. Although, of course, it is broken, so it does not.'

Emily is sitting with her foot near my leg. She kicks me hard in the shin for no reason and when I look to her she is crossing her eyes, trying to make me laugh. It would be mean to laugh at our mother and so I scowl at her instead.

The Nude Maja

When I open my office door John is still outside. There is an awkwardness. He shifts his weight from foot to foot and his gaze is furtive. He looks everywhere but at me. The pages of his sketchbook protrude from his folder. It looks as if he might drop them at any moment.

'Okay.' I step aside and he sidles past me. The sole of his taped-up shoe flaps. He is tall and he hunches. It gives him a cowed look.

'Hi.' John sits in the comfy couch opposite my desk and picks up the nearest book, turning the pages so quickly that it seems he is not looking at the pictures at all.

When the book is shut and resting in his lap he glances up at me. 'I like the way Goya uses a single source of light.'

'Did you read that somewhere?'

'No. I just noticed.' He glances up at the wall and nods. 'Your sister does that too. One light source. It's very dramatic.'

I nod. John shrugs. 'Just an observation.'

'We all have our habits.'

'Yes,' he says. 'You backlight things as if there is a lamp hidden somewhere behind them. Subtle. But effective.'

'What do you want, John?'

John shifts on the leather couch. He is round, round-bellied, round-shouldered, moon face gazing up at me half terror, half expectation. I am reminded of puppies when they get wind of food, wide-eyed hope and fear all at once.

'To go look at your etchings?'

This is a joke, of course, but he says it without a smile. He is all hunched over himself and his irises are small and dark in the wide white stare. It breaks my heart to look at him, his eager expectation.

'I thought we were going to stop all that.'

'Were we?'

'You're my student, John.'

He leans forward and opens the heavy cover of the art book. He flicks past Manet, Raphael, Picasso.

'You know Goya went deaf, right? I don't remember what caused that.'

'Cholera.'

'Right. Well I was wondering if that's when he changed his relationship to light. I was wondering why your sister shines a spotlight on her subject, head on, like from a car. Even when the light should be from the fire on his back or the girl with the burning hands, instead it's head on like a car is rocketing towards her about to collide. What made her do that? Did she always do that? Even when she was little?' He turns to look at my sister's paintings, leans towards them as if listening for them to answer.

'Or is it something to do with the illness?' I say, perhaps a little too sharply. People are always trying to diagnose my sister through her art.

'Maybe. I wasn't trying to…I didn't…'

'No, John. She always did that.'

'So, then you do this thing in your paintings where it seems like natural light, daylight, but there's a halo or something, the hair outlined. Just a tiny glow and I bet people don't notice it often.'

'People have to see the paintings to notice something about them.'

'Come on. You've exhibited.'

He is right, I have exhibited once or twice. Before. Thumbnail reviews. No real feedback. Shouting into the wind.

'You're very observant,' I say, and it is nice how he blushes. I have always liked that about him.

'I liked your work today.'

'She was nice.'

'The model?'

'Yes.'

'Mmm.'

'You just don't like her because she's pretty.' Which is probably true. 'You hate them because you think they're more attractive than you. Which is not true.'

'Yeah, and flattery is going to get you a glimpse at my etchings.'

'Oh. Isn't it?'

I sink into the chair at my desk. There are wheels on it and I push off and roll back and let the chair thud against the wall. It is a habit and I only catch myself doing it when it is too late. He grins and flicks through pages till he spots the one he is looking for. He holds the book up as if he were showing it to a child. *The Nude Maja.*

'She looks a bit like you don't you think?'

He stares at the picture intently, scratches his generous belly. 'Except you'd have a big scar all down your front.'

'No. Five little scars.'

'Five?'

'Yeah. Who would have thought keyhole meant keyholes. Five of them.'

I notice his hand stretch out as if he would touch my knee, but I'm a long way away from him. He taps his fingers on his own thigh instead, a little gesture of comfort that I might have shared in.

He is a nice boy. I kick my chair closer to him.

'I would like to come over to your place,' he says, peering down into his lap where he folds his fingers into a little fence.

'To see my etchings.'

'No. To kiss you. Make out a little bit. Drink tea after.'

I press my fingers against my lips. They smell like a hospital. I wonder why this is so. I wonder if the anaesthetic is still in me somehow, sweating out of my pores. I am suddenly very tired.

'I said I wouldn't do that anymore.'

He shrugs. 'Sure, but we say these things. We mean them at the time.'

I lean forward into the hug of my arms. My desk smells like linseed oil and I am suddenly longing for home. When I look up, there is such an open, expectant look in John's eyes that I am a child once more, and nothing can be wrong with what we are about to do.

'I am forty years old,' I say, more to remind myself than to inform him.

'I know,' he says. 'I'm twenty-three. I am an adult. I make my own choices. I would like to go back to your place if you let me. I would like to kiss you again.'

We mustn't sleep with our students. Some of the male lecturers do it. I have suspected, seen them out at dinner or letting the kids out of their cars first thing in the morning. I have always judged them harshly for it. It is immoral, I say. How can you be objective? They shouldn't be allowed to mark their work, I say.

I let John ride in my car. I open the passenger door and feel the quick sinking of the car as he steps into it. I remember the weight of him bearing down onto my chest, his arms straining to keep the bulk of his body from pressing the breath out of me.

People will see us leaving together. Other students, other lecturers. When they confront me with this I will tell them that I am teaching him to stretch a canvas. Last time I did not need to make up such a story. Last time I gave him an address and drove home to pace and fret, wishing that he would become lost and abandon our meeting altogether, then worrying that this was exactly what had happened and sinking into the foetid pit of my own insecurities.

I am afraid that I am too old and too ugly for him. I am not a good enough artist. He would never abandon me if I were as accomplished as my sister. He only became interested in me because of this sibling connection and the crazy brush with fame it affords him.

This does not matter now. I slip behind the wheel and there

is the smell of him, sweat, socks, oil paint, the vague chemical reek of the photo lab, a doughy masculine warmth that will obliterate the other smells when I remove his clothing. It is a smell that is so strong it should be off-putting but as I breathe in I am suddenly wet with desire.

He stands awkwardly in the lounge room, the site of our first transgression. He sits on the edge of the couch where I lay him back and slipped his penis into my mouth and swallowed the sticky sharp flavour that I hadn't tasted in years.

I bring him a glass of wine and sip my own a little too quickly and I know that this is going to end with too little from him and too much from me but even that kind of unevenness is better than this awkward perching. I lean forward and when I am close enough he kisses me and I am too distracted by the complications of assessment time. The fact that he is my best student. The most talented artist that has sat in my classes. But if I mark him high as I have always done there will now be an edge of doubt. This is the ethical dilemma I have made for myself.

His lips are full and soft. The kiss is damp without being wet and it takes a long time for him to softly part his mouth and allow me to find his tongue there. It is a kiss so full of excitement and desire that it is easy to lose the facts of the situation to the sheer physical pleasure of it. I am without guilt, and this alone makes me guilty. I am aware that he is younger than I am, fresher, more energetic. I am aware that my kisses are a pale substitute for the intensity of flesh and fire that he so admires in my sister's work. When we are both naked and his head is dipped towards my breast, I see him glance up and beyond me. There is an image on my wall that my sister painted when she was fifteen. A raw and passionate coupling of anonymous bodies. I know that he is looking at the painting, his penis rising against my thigh and this small distraction is enough to make me want him more. I shift onto his lap and he is inside me. I have not forgotten to put a condom on him, I am not so morally bereft as to risk our health and safety. It is an easy enough thing to lift one leg and clamber over and onto him and from this angle he will be able to look over my shoulder and bask in the raw eroticism of my sister's work.

The little injection of jealousy sends a sharp contraction through my loins. When it has begun it is impossible to avoid the slide over into the disappointment of a premature climax. I come so quickly that it is almost without pleasure.

Without the heat of desire it all seems so much more sordid. My bra abandoned on the rug, the stiff cups looking huge and somehow parental, the slight dark stain in the crotch of my knickers. I am aware too, that I am still sore and that my scars stand out a vivid red against my flabby pale stomach. The whole of my belly is even more swollen than it usually is. I am a wreck.

I ease myself off him although I know he is not even close to his own climax. I roll the condom off and dip my head into his lap. There is the terrible oceanic smell of me. I try, impossibly, to breathe through my mouth and suck him at the same time. This smell is why I have not had anyone go down on me since I was a teenager.

I know that if I meet this boy again, the pattern will have been set and we will be back here, me on my knees hoping that he will come quicker than he did the last time, wondering how long the tired muscles of my mouth will be able to continue at this pace.

Wondering if this time I will have to gag when he comes into my mouth. Wondering how I will be able to swallow without smelling the reek of my own crotch. Knowing that other women do not smell as strongly as I do. Knowing that my sister is all candy apple and fresh baked bread and I am all day-old fish and seaweed caked in salt. I wish it was over. I wish it had never begun. I am wishing myself back to whatever went wrong in the first place that made it possible for me to be here now and with him. I am thinking about my sister when I should be here enjoying the moments when I am risking my career to be on my knees in front of this young man.

There is a sharp pain in my gut but I keep at my task with a fierce tenacity. When it is done, I swallow quickly and slouch back on the couch. I place my hand under my ribs, imagining that I have torn open the wound and must be bleeding all over the rug, but it is still just a sore red puckered slit. Five bright scars without a drop of blood. I look at my stomach with a kind of disappointment.

'I'm sorry.' He is a nice boy. His concern is palpable. 'Did I hurt you? I'm sorry if I hurt you.'

'No.' I let him cup my chin in his hand and I do like him enormously. He is the best artist I have ever taught. He is almost the equal of my sister. 'It's fine. Thank you.'

'Thank you? It's me that should be thanking you.' And he kisses me with those wonderfully soft and gentle lips and suddenly I no longer regret what we have done, and the only thing I will regret is this lack of regret. I know in this moment that I am the bad sister, not Emily. It is easy to point the finger at Emily. But it is me. This insidious evil that pretends to be the nice girl in the family.

H is for Horse

I have my role to play and I take it very seriously. It is my job to make the first offering to the horse. There are words to say and I have said them every day since this particular ritual began. *Saddle up,* I say and *here boy, there boy, eat from my hand.* For a while I also had to say *take to the bit* but, because we have no bit, Emily decided I shouldn't say it at all.

That was a few weeks ago now and all I have are the two lines and one handful of lucerne. The kitchen scraps are to be left for Emily, because Flame is Emily's horse. She speaks to the horse in Elvish, and, because I have never managed to master the language no matter how often we play that game, I am never sure what she is saying. It doesn't matter. Flame knows it is her and that she is the one who owns him.

I am sure he can smell us when we are crossing the paddock. We have fifty acres and the land is uneven and boggy in places. There is a dry creek bed on our land but, unless it is raining heavily, I can't tell where the creek starts and finishes. We trudge over high ground and low ground and by the time we get to the fence line we are ripe with sweat.

She whistles three times. This is the start of it, and then, 'Tch tch tch tch.' We call him simultaneously, clicking our tongues against our teeth. Emily taught me how to do this and sometimes I think that, although I cannot whistle, I am almost better at the galloping sound than she is.

He really is the most magnificent creature I have ever seen. Emily says that no one loves Flame except us and yet he is always well groomed. His flanks glow as if he has only just been brushed. His mane is never matted. When he runs a shudder ripples through his muscular body. When he stamps his legs twitch. He smells spicy, his chestnut coat warm and clean but pungent all the same.

He is still nodding his head as if in agreement when I step up to the wire and play my part. A bow first, careful not to get in the way of his powerful nose which has knocked me in the head several times, once even causing me to bite my tongue. Then there are the lines I must speak, and Flame waits patiently for me to say them. I put the lucerne on my hand and am careful to hold it flat. I know that he could bite my fingers by accident. I suppose Emily told me this but I have no memory of when she said it. I hold my hand flat and do not flinch. I won't let Emily see that I am scared of his searching lips and big teeth but I always am.

When she takes her place and bows and steps forward, I wipe the horse spit on the back of my skirt. The air is so still and I lift my hair off my neck where it is damp with sweat and sticking to my skin.

I see him out of the corner of my eye, just a scrap of movement over on the ridge. Of course we have never climbed through the fence or ventured onto the neighbour's property but I always imagined just more of the same flat scrubby paddocks stretching away over the hill, right out to the horizon line. I look towards the movement, squint into the sun and it is a person, a boy, just another farm boy in a flannelette shirt like all the other farm boys we see loitering outside the shop or waiting for the school bus on the side of the road when our grandmother takes us with her to town.

He is walking towards us and I tap my sister on her hip. She turns towards me and she scowls. This is the most important part of her day and I am interrupting her.

I tilt my head and squint towards the boy, who is closer now. He walks with a lilt, shifting from side to side with each step, a swagger. I am reminded of gunslingers, gangsters, prison guards that I have read about in novels. His hair is cropped too short and his skull glares out beneath the stubble. He has the kind of features that mark him as a local. A shared thick jaw, a heavy brow. Emily says it is interbreeding, cousins marrying cousins, and it is hard to disagree when you see his face and it could be any face on any boy from town. He has that same sneer too, or maybe that is just the kind of look that my family inspires. We so rarely see ourselves through the eyes of others and it is odd to notice how wary of us they are, wary and contemptuous, fascinated and confused.

He swaggers up to the fence line and grabs a lock of Flame's hair in his fist and I can feel Emily flinch beside me. He hooks the horse's neck up with his arm and slaps him gently, an upended headlock, and Flame just snorts and nods and stamps a little which is exactly what he does when we visit with him.

'You're not feeding Joey anything are you?'

Joey.

Emily's hand becomes a fist but her face remains impassive. Flame's jaw is still working at the last of a carrot.

'Is there a problem?'

We never talk to other kids, or rarely. I am not sure I could do it as easily as she is. I look down at my feet and I know this makes me seem shy but I am not. I am just unused to strangers, a strange boy this close to us without our grandmother around to intervene. There is a buzz of excitement, I feel as if anything could happen. No windows to lock tight against this stranger. He could so easily rob us or beat us, or kill us or worse. Because if a boy touches us it will be worse than death even. He settles his weight between his splayed feet, shifting from one to the other. He watches us through narrowed eyes, distrustful.

'Yeah well, Joey is my horse and I need to know what he's eating. There are things a horse shouldn't eat although you wouldn't know that I suppose.'

'And why wouldn't we know that?'

My sister is short but she seems taller than this boy. It must be something about the way her back is so straight, her arms tight with anger, chin raised. She looks tall and strong and I inch closer, inside the comforting bubble of her fury.

He shrugs. 'You know. You, with your mum and your gran and all that.'

She stares at him for a moment. I see her head move as she literally looks him up and down. She reaches out then and Flame leans forward, nudging the cup of her hand. The horse licks at her fingers and the boy yanks suddenly at the animal's mane. Flame whinnies, stamps.

'Don't touch my horse.'

'Horses don't belong to people,' she tells him. Her calm is terrifying.

'Yes they do. I don't know what dumb bullshit you have in your religion but in normal religion it's that animals were put on this earth for people. Not the other way round.'

She laughs, a little snigger of air and he spits on the ground at his feet.

'Exactly what religion do you think we are?'

I watch him swell to his right height. He inflates like a balloon, one short sharp breath after another. He is big, broad shouldered, his jaw looks too big for his face.

'I don't know. Vegetarianism—'

'—is not a religion.'

'Mormons.'

She shakes her head defiantly.

'Freak religion then. Cause you are freaks. Everyone says you are.'

My sister stands straight and strong, an immovable force. For a moment I see a small version of our grandmother standing there, terrifying in her certainty. 'This is not your horse. I have never seen you here before. You don't even live here.'

'Yeah,' he says, his shoulders slumping a little, some of the air taken out of him. 'I live here. Except when I'm at boarding school, eh?'

'So go back to boarding school, eh?'

I put my hand on her arm and tug at it. Our house is so close. I can see it from here. I take a step towards home but she doesn't move. The boy knows he is being mocked, but he seems uncertain what he should do about it. He turns to face Flame's glistening flank and pats it as if to prove that he has the right to do this when we have not.

'Stop touching my horse. I might catch something off yous.'

My sister speaks then and I feel the blood rising into my cheeks. I listen in horror to the soft syllables she learned from the alphabet in the back of *The Lord of the Rings*. I listen to the sounds slipping easily off her tongue and I cringe. It is not just that she is speaking Elvish in front of a stranger, it is that she is proving him right.

It would be difficult living next door to the freaks. He is right about that. Real girls would go to their town school and eat the bad food and go to the rodeo. Real girls would wear normal clothes and say 'eh' at the end of their sentences and use words like 'yous' and 'chicks'. I float somewhere outside myself. Looking down there is a girl in a hand-sewn dress with a bad home haircut and a dumb ritual with a horse that doesn't belong to her. I step away from my sister, I edge back towards home.

The boy spits in the earth once more. And then an astonishing thing happens. He slips up and onto the back of the horse. His fingers laced in the mane, he lifts and throws his leg over the horse's back and Flame does nothing but a quick jog forward. I can feel my sister stiffen beside me. The idea that someone can ride him, that this boy rides him.

'Just don't feed my horse, freak,' and he turns and trots away from us.

She spits words at him. I am not sure exactly what she is saying but it is some kind of curse. She is our grandmother exactly. It is there in the way she stands her ground, speaking in a made-up language that will mark her as a freak more firmly

42

than anything she might have said in English.

'Let's go home,' I whisper, but she ignores me, standing stiff and as tall as she can until the boy has cantered off with Flame up and over the ridge out of sight.

She turns towards me then but without looking at me. I am a disappointment to her. I am weak and my retreat has proved this. I see my grandmother's terrible disapproval and wish there were something I could do to make it right. She stalks past me and I have to jog a little to keep pace.

Oma in Hospital

Oma pins me with the sharp needles of her eyes. I can feel it. My hands itch when she stares at them, my feet ache. I imagine she can smell John on me. This, more than anything, makes me sit uncomfortably on the edge of the plastic chair at the other side of the room. I am straight-backed and prim, my skirt smoothed down over my knees. I might be seven years old again, waiting for home-school to begin. I am like this with her, always polite, always sitting straight as the back of the wooden chair. Good sister. Praise for me, consternation for Emily.

Now that there is only one of us to visit her, my grandmother frowns with half of her face. The other side of it is slack, rubbery, barely flinching as she catches sight of me. Her good hand taps. They've let her nails grow long. I imagine the struggle that the nurses must have with her, harried looking young men and women staring at me sideways on the rare occasions of my visits. She bunches her fingers together so they resemble the beak of some avian predator. The tapping makes her seem hungry somehow. I sit on her left side where she can easily see me. On the right she sometimes forgets I am there at all, startled at my reappearance whenever I walk across the room to pour her a glass of water.

The tapping sets my teeth grinding. She would chide me about this, but her words are jumbled up inside her head. The nurses tell me that she refuses to speak at all, preferring silence to the possibility of error.

'My operation went okay,' I say, to interrupt her tapping. She pauses, her hand raised, the fingers pressed together.

'The doctor said the stone was the size of an Easter egg.'

I know she's not concerned with my minor ailments. She doesn't speak but I can hear her clearly enough. *You still have your words. You can use both your hands. You walk without a limp. You can read words on a page.*

'So, there were three men having their gall bladders out at the same time. Same operation as me, right?'

Her fingers tap down on the metal table, a ticking of talons, a marking of time.

'And, the doctor leaned over and whispered to me that my gall stone was the biggest.'

Pride. Talking yourself up. I wish I hadn't said anything at all. My straight good-girl back sags down just a little. I resist the urge to check my watch. There is tea and I sip it, drawing the minutes out. I will not have to speak for a while. I sit and listen to the tapping gradually quicken. Normally, I would talk about work next, but John is there in front of my office door smiling in that disarming manner, waiting like a puppy to be let in.

He is new in my life. The last time I visited I spoke about him, my best student, an exciting talent. Perhaps she realised there was a transgression brewing before I even knew it myself. I feel her silence like a cold finger poking around inside my head, finding John there hiding among my secrets. As children we thought she knew everything. Now I wonder if she knows about John or, and I realise this with a sudden cold shock, if she knows that Emily has called. I can feel myself itching to confess. Emily would not want me to tell. Emily would want this to be our secret. The tea is weak and milky. This is how they serve their tea. Inside that silent body I imagine that she is furious. Only her fingernails betray her.

I drink in silence. I look up and smile, a wan lie of a smile without teeth. Eventually I stand and the tapping stops, her fingers poised, waiting for me to leave. I kiss the slack side of her face where she will not feel my lips trembling. I wave to her neglectful eye.

Bad granddaughter, liar. A disappointment of a woman leaving awkwardly, hip colliding with the wall. I leave the ward quickly, tripping over nothing, righting myself against the information counter.

'Nice visit?'

The nurse is a little younger than I am. His muscular shoulders pull tight against his uniform.

I nod. My face is a mask of guilt.

'She's very…wilful, your grandmother.' I imagine this is the kindest of the words he has for her. I feel embarrassed.

'Formidable,' I offer and he nods knowingly. I wonder how my Oma has demonstrated her power without the aid of speech or writing. Perhaps I should feel a camaraderie with the nurse but instead I just feel guilty again. I try to match his smile before I turn and flee into the heat of the bare car park.

Safely away, I realise how tight my shoulders have been. I stretch my neck, one side then the other. A crackle of relief, an audible relaxing.

When I settle into the car I can smell John, a small reminder of his skin. I find it comforting. I am taking deep breaths, drinking in the odour that has somehow impregnated itself into the upholstery. It is unsettling, this longing for someone you should not be with. It frightens me a little, which in itself is arousing. I sit for a moment.

I turn the key. The car shudders but does not start. I try again and there's more mechanical chugging. For a moment I imagine it is my grandmother, the insidious finger of her willpower stopping the car dead, but when I turn the key a third time the car starts. Not the witchy power of our Oma, then. If it was her she would never let me leave at all.

Phone Voice

Emily is in the lounge room. Our grandmother is in her study, the smell of turps and glue so strong that I become faint with it as I sneak past her door. I am still groggy from an early afternoon nap. Emily calls me a baby for having naps but when I try to stay awake to spend more time with her I am too tired to follow her games and she calls me stupid and sometimes I am so tired that she makes me cry.

Today I steady myself on the wall and stumble towards the lounge room. Our mother is usually there somewhere, hovering near the window, but today I notice her absence. The first surprise. She must be in her bedroom, which is rare at this time in the day.

Emily is sitting beside the phone. At first it looks like she is speaking into it, but when I take a step into the room I see that she is hunched over it, her ear pressed up against the back of the earpiece, her mouth near the back of the mouthpiece. She is whispering, 'Yes, yes, yes, okay. Are you sure? Ah huh. Ah huh. Ah huh.'

It is like a conversation but one where I can only hear the uninteresting part. The good bit of it is going on in Emily's head. It must be a game. It is a game to fill in the time till I am awake. Now I am here I crook my fingers up against my head, my thumb to my ear, my little finger to my mouth. I walk quietly into the room thinking that she will be so surprised and pleased to have someone to play this game with.

'All right then I am back again now,' I say into my pretend telephone and watch her snap her head up sharply like a startled bird, her beak in the air, her eyes glazed as if she is having trouble focusing on the room around her.

'So what were we talking about again?' I say, quite loudly into my telephonic hand.

'You've scared him,' she says sharply. 'You've scared him away.'

And she seems truly upset by this. She puts her hand onto the telephone as if it were an animal that needs calming.

'Who?'

She glances at the phone and then back in my direction and she is coming back into herself. Her expression changes from one of bewilderment to the hard, one-sided smile my sister often has.

'You're too young,' she says, 'you wouldn't understand.' She reaches up to her hair, tightens the ribbon she has tied there and makes her way out through the back door. With the sound of it slapping, faster, coming to rest after a dozen little reprimands, I am alone in the lounge room. The phone is still warm from where her head rested against it. I lift it out of its cradle and listen. Nothing, of course. There was never anyone on the other end, but there is something in the flat, empty tone that makes me wonder, and listening closely for the longest time, it is as if I can hear someone breathing, regularly, in time with the note of disconnection.

It is true. I can hear it. Someone is there, hiding behind the idea that it is a dead line. Someone is listening to me, breathing out when the low beep starts, breathing in when it finishes. The more I listen the clearer the breathing becomes. A cold wave creeps up the back of my neck and I slam the phone back into its cradle. I should walk away now. There are goose-bumps crawling along my upper arms. I am cold despite the warm air. I lean close to the phone and even though it is set in place, I whisper into the back of the mouthpiece.

'Hello?' And then when I hear nothing, 'Who are you?'

Now would be the time for a voice to come to me and I am tensed and ready for it.

'Who are you?'

I pick up the phone again and I am afraid. But Emily has been here before me, Emily is brave and I will be brave too. If Emily has found a friend hidden here then I will dig him out. I will not be separated from Emily's games. I will not be a stranger to her friends.

'Who are you?' It is just a whisper and I am so tight in my limbs that my leg is turning to pins and needles with my fear.

No sound, just the flat low tone and yes, there, the breathing. Someone breathing through it.

'It's okay to talk to me,' I say to the sound. 'I'm her sister.'

Tone, and breathing. I listen for a while and then when I hear the creak of the floorboards I put the phone back in its cradle and scuttle onto the couch. It is our mother, the zombie shuffle of her feet, tentative on the floorboards. For once I wish she would settle in the seat beside me as she sometimes does, but instead she stands at the window and I imagine she is watching Emily instead of me. It is ridiculous, but it seems that maybe they are keeping a secret from me, Emily and our mother and whoever it is on the phone. I stand and creep towards her, hovering beside my mother where I can see out to the back garden. My sister is nowhere to be seen.

Séance

'You know this is ridiculous.' I am wearing the wrong thing of
course. I changed four times and still I made the wrong decision.
I am overdressed. It is a pretty frock, possibly my prettiest, a flatter-
ing black and pulled tight and low at the breasts, taking the
attention away from my stomach. It is the first thing he noticed,
I could tell. He stood at my door and his eyes kept darting to my
breasts in a way that made me blush a little and made me want
to slip out of the dress quite a lot. Still, he didn't reach for them,
no soft kisses, just an awkward shuffling of his feet as he waited
for me to get my purse.

   This is our first date, if you can call it a date. I suppose he made
an effort. He is wearing a jacket. I have rarely seen him in a jacket.
This is an old one from a suit that is too big for him and he has
matched it with his uniform old jeans and taped-up shoes. His
hair has been brushed which is another sign of the care he
has taken. It is a date, I suppose. I should not be going on a date
with him.

'Do you promise there will be no uni people there? No friends of friends? Or even friends of friends of friends?'

'Do you want to wear a disguise? I think we have time for you to put on a fake beard or maybe just a moustache.'

'You know what I mean.'

'Do you have a coat? You're going to get cold if you don't cover your chest.'

'I'm overdressed, aren't I?'

'No! You are not overdressed. You are beautiful. You have beautiful breasts.'

'Too much cleavage?'

'Never. How can you say that? Too much cleavage? Whoever heard of such a thing?'

My smile is my reward for him. I should be laughing because he likes to make me laugh but I am too tense to laugh. In the car I ask him if there will be anybody else the same age as me.

'I went to high school with these people,' he says. 'Maybe someone repeated a year or two but I don't think anyone was held back that long.'

'I'll drop you there. I should just stay home. Really.'

'Can you just shut up? Really?'

I miss the turn and we have to negotiate a series of one-way streets before I finally get us back on the right path.

'You know I'm proud to be seen with you,' he tells me suddenly. 'I wouldn't want to take you if I wasn't.'

'Okay.'

When we pull up outside the low brick house he asks me about my grandmother. 'How was she?'

'We are about to go into this party aren't we?'

'Dinner party.'

'Dinner party then.'

'Yes.'

'And you ask me now about my grandmother?'

'Long story, huh?'

I wrench the handbrake on and put the car into gear. It is a steep hill and I wonder if I should find a brick. I glance around the perfectly manicured suburban gardens. The car will be fine. I lock the doors and take a deep breath. He puts out his elbow like a leading man from a forties movie and I take it with that same thin smile.

'You look nice,' he says, and kisses me lightly on the cheek.

The truth is my grandmother did not look well. She has lost weight. When I was free of the angry tapping of her finger and the implied threat of her half-scowl I realised how frail she actually seemed. The right side of her body has been thin and slack-skinned since the stroke. I am used to a certain emaciated drag, but it has been too long between visits. She seemed old.

Still, in the safety of retrospect it would be easy to misread exhaustion for a softening. *You have a boyfriend.* All the accusations were there in her silence. Even if she could speak there would be no questions. Oma never asked questions. *You must not take your students as boyfriends. You are a disappointment to me. You should be smarter than this.*

She would never approve. Not even I approve. The only way to hide John from her is to see her less often. I will abandon her, the last fragment of my family, for someone who is just over half my age. The weight of guilt makes me slump-shouldered.

I wonder if John's friends will see me the way I saw my own grandmother, a physical reminder of the grave we are all slouching towards.

He knocks. I slip my hand off his arm and his fingers reach for mine so that we are holding hands when the door opens.

The young man at the door is a child, a fresh-faced Aryan boy. He has a thick leather band around his wrist and a short leather jacket to match. I did not even know that this was a style. Certainly none of the art students wear leather wristbands and the jacket is padded at the shoulders like the jackets I remember from the eighties.

'Well,' he says and he is looking at me. Pale blue eyes and a stare that could cut glass. He is smiling and he sways just slightly and I realise that he is a little drunk and we are only just arriving. 'Welcome,' he says and John shrugs.

'Bec, Charles, Charles, Bec.' The boy tilts his head to one side. His gaze is too intense and I am relieved when another, taller boy with shaggy brown hair and a wide jaw leans over his shoulder and takes my hand and shakes it.

'And Andy,' John tells me. 'But I went to school with Charles not Andy, which is a shame because Charles used to beat me up and Andy would have been nicer to me.'

'What? No.' Charles leans into Andy's shoulder, staring thoughtfully at the eaves and I realise they are a couple. 'Oh maybe that one time. But you have to admit…'

'No,' John chuckles. 'You have to admit. You were horrible. You did have to admit it.'

'Well yes, that one time but only that one time and I so could have beaten you up on plenty more occasions than that.'

'You know how boys are,' Andy tells me. 'They hit someone if they have a crush on them.'

'No, we wrestle,' Charles corrects him and reaches out to jostle playfully with John.

Inside there are too many people to remember. I am introduced quickly and just as quickly forget everybody's names. They are all in their twenties. Some of them, like Charles, look almost like teenagers; others, like Andy, might be a little older, maybe thirty at a stretch. I am overdressed. The girls all wear short skirts and tights or jeans. The boys are more formal in jackets and coats and one boy, a pretty Asian boy who looks no more than sixteen, is even wearing a skinny tie.

There is an open bottle of vodka on the table and they pour shots from it, some of them mixing with cranberry or orange juice. Charles pours a straight shot and knocks it back in a flamboyant toast to the mother of all goats as Andy brings a great roasted beast to the table, the legs still on it and sticking up straight towards the ceiling. It looks inedible, but the serving that arrives on my plate is surprisingly tender, with a pleasantly charred flavour. The meal is nice, spiced vegetables, hot bread cut in thick slices to soak up the juices. I glean from the conversation that Charles and Andy are known for their culinary expertise. It seems it is an honour to be on their guest list. John puts his hand on my knee and I notice one of the girls watching the gesture with a slightly confused expression. She might have thought I was his mother, or at least an aunt.

They are talking about some movie they have all seen, something about a vampire, but not the vampire one that is really bad and terribly uncool apparently. This other vampire movie is less bad, but still quite awful and not worth the price of a ticket although it seems that they have all forked out the $9.50 to see it, or whatever a student movie ticket is worth these days. Someone calls my name and I turn too quickly and my neck clicks painfully. I didn't realise I was quite this tense and I put my hand to my neck as if I am scratching it, pressing my fingers into the tender spot until it hurts less.

'Sorry? What was that?'

'I was just wondering where you met John.'

'Bali,' John tells the young girl without flinching. 'Over a pina colada and a game of craps.'

The girl is very pretty, delicate pixie face and long blonde hair that she keeps folding back behind her ear in a self-conscious, slightly flirtatious manner. When she screws up her nose and mouth her pixie look becomes slightly rattish. She will not age well. It is an unkind thought, but it is a comforting one.

'Art school,' I say and she seems interested. She leans forward.

'What strand are you studying?'

'Sculpture.'

'Oh cool. What, like clay?'

'Polymers,' I tell her quickly, surprised by my own ability to lie. 'Industrial materials. I want to fill the art gallery with poly-styrene, make the punters cut their way into the exhibition with a hot knife.'

'Oh cool,' she says.

'Actually that is very cool,' John looks at me warily.

'Will they let you do that?' the girl asks and I shake my head.

'Nah, probably not. Shame.'

'Yeah, it is a shame,' John says, 'because that actually would be excellent. Dibs.' I shake my head, a warning, and he winks.

There is sharp ringing laughter, which sounds surprisingly like someone is clanging a dinner bell. When we turn to look there is a board spread out on the table. Letters of the alphabet fanning out along the circumference of a circle. The words *No, Yes, Maybe* and *Re-phrase your question*, mark the corners of the board outside the circle. It is a ouija board. I have never seen one before but I have read about them. There is a pentacle in the centre of the board and a triangle of what looks like stone but is probably plastic perched in the middle. I feel my neck tightening yet again. I lean over to John.

'Maybe we should go,' I whisper and he turns to me with such startled wide-eyed despondency that I settle back down in my seat.

'We must all hold hands,' Charles tells us. 'Clear your minds of all scepticism. You lot will skew the results with your cynical little brains sending out bad magnetism.'

There are a few nervous titters from the guests and I feel a small clammy palm slip into mine. I turn to see the pretty young pixie smiling shyly at me before giving her concentration over to the master of ceremonies. On the other side John squeezes my hand and I squeeze his back.

'You know I saw a ghost once.' This from a young man with severe square glasses and a shaved head.

'That what happened to your hair, Stan?'

Some laughter and Stan lets go of his neighbours' hands briefly before Charles tuts at him and he reconnects the circle.

'You may laugh, but sometimes you just don't know what

you're playing with when you call up the demons or what have you.'

There is some laughter but they are shushed by the pixie girl.

'I agree,' says Pixie, 'although we should totally do this now and everything, but if you get an evil spirit it might be impossible to put him back in his bottle.'

'That's a genie, douchebag.'

'*Paranormal Activity*,' says someone else and a few people make an appreciative sound.

'That was so awesome. The first one.'

'Hideous.'

'Awesome.'

'*The Exorcist* is pretty frightening still.'

I shouldn't have spoken. Three people splutter with laughter and another one shouts 'Fuck me Jesus!' and lets his eyes turn upward, revealing a big globe of milky white in each socket.

'No it's not,' John assures me and I know my cheeks are going red. 'Well, not anymore. It's interesting, but there are too many references in *The Simpsons* for us to be scared by it. I think it's a generational thing.'

My cheeks are blazing and I put my head down and try to creep my fingers out of John's hand. He holds them tighter and presses his knee against mine.

'I didn't mean anything by that,' he whispers and I shake my head hoping that he will take the hint and stop talking at all.

'If you are there. Let us know,' says Charles. He touches the stone lightly with his finger. Andy has another corner and the third is held by a short boy with a Scottish accent who I haven't been introduced to.

'Did you feel anything?' the Scotsman asks.

'On the ouija board?' asks Andy, leering suggestively.

'Of course.'

'Ah, well no then, I didn't feel anything,' and there is a little laughter, more nervous this time.

'If you are with us. Give us a sign.'

Silence now, I feel a tightness in my chest. Something is wrong. I am sick. It is a cramp perhaps, or maybe my heart. What if I were to have a heart attack in front of all of John's friends? Old lady passes out at dinner table. I try to swallow but my throat is dry.

'Are you there? Is anyone there?'

I lean towards John. 'I have to leave.'

Just a whisper, and he turns his head towards my ear and says, 'Not just yet.'

They are waiting. Everyone is waiting. There is the kind of silence that you get when the room is full of people, little scraping sounds, the creak of a chair, the sound of a shoe squeaking against the polished boards.

'We know you are there.'

And in the silence I know it is true. I know he is here. I can hear him. I can hear him breathing, and the moment I hear it I cannot unhear it. There is the regular breath in, breath out, breath in, breath out. I hold my own breath to be sure but his breathing does not falter.

The stone shifts slowly towards the corner of the board. Yes.

'Yes,' Charles interprets for the rest of us. 'Yes you are here with us now.'

'He is here,' I say. But it wasn't him that moved the stone. That was Charles's finger or Andy's or the Scottish boy's. A simple parlour game, but he is here with us anyway, just like he was there with me when I was a child, on every occasion that I picked up the phone. The sound of his breathing in counterpoint to the flat beeping of the telephone. A disengaged signal but the boy was there anyway, and he is here now.

'Stop it.' I shout so suddenly that even I am startled by it. He is here. I can hear him. I can almost see him. I trip back over the chair, fall, a plate clatters to the floor, the skittering of its many pieces on the floor. I can almost see him. I hold my hands over my eyes as if this will stop him from appearing.

'This is bullshit,' the pixie girl shrieks. I have startled her with my sudden outburst. I stand and wrestle my fingers away from John. Everyone is staring at me. Someone laughs then stops and the room returns to silence. I can hear my heart thudding in a chest so tight that my own body might suffocate me.

'I'm sorry John,' breathless. 'I'm so sorry. I have to go.'

'Hey, hey…' John stands.

'Stay here,' I tell him. 'I'll get a cab.'

But he follows me out. I am certain he has signalled to his friends, his palms raised perhaps, his finger circling his ear, whatever it is, it takes only a minute because he is trotting beside me by the time I reach the car.

'Oh darl,' he says and touches my face and it is only then that I realise there are tears on it.

'God. I'm sorry.'

'It's okay,' he tries to comfort me.

'That was a disaster.'

'It's okay. Really it's okay. It was just a silly joke game.'

'And I'm the joke.'

'No.'

I nod and he gathers me up into his hug where I feel warmer and safer but not completely safe.

'What happened back there?' he asks when I have settled enough to start the car.

'I freaked out.'

'Sure. But what happened?'

'Old stuff. Dumb stuff. I'm sorry I embarrassed you.'

'Honestly it's okay. They were all drunk. You probably made their night. Demonic possession, they'll call it. Charles will want you at all their dinners from now on.'

'I can't go back.'

'Sure you can. They'll all be rotten drunk. Half of them won't remember anything about tonight. The other half will be embarrassed about vomiting in Charles's pebble garden. Someone always vomits in Charles's pebble garden.'

'Yeah?'

'Sure they do. It's like a running gag at that place.'

He puts his hand on my knee.

There was no one there, of course. He is right. It was just a bunch of kids playing a silly, harmless game.

'I was a million years older than everyone anyway.'

'Yeah,' he shrugs, 'there's that. You can beat yourself up about that if you like.'

He really does know how to make me smile. When I have put the car in gear I rest my hand briefly on his knee and he squeezes mine.

'Come on,' he says, 'let's blow this crazy popsicle stand.'

And so we do.

Madness

'Stop!'

I am facing the wall, the invisible line that must not be crossed. I do not look at her naked and she does not look at me. The masking tape on the ground dividing her side of the room from mine is a solid wall.

'Stop! Now!'

When she shouts at me it is like an earthquake, fault lines in the invisible wall spreading out, the sound of her voice a wrecking ball. The wall crumbles. I have already put my jeans on, which is lucky because I am only half naked, the T-shirt clutched to that horrible embarrassment of my chest. I have breasts. There is no use denying this. What might once have been a mistake, a trick of the light, a glance at the wrong angle, is now an undeniable fact. My breasts are large enough to have a small overhang. You are saggy if you can hold a pencil up under them, my sister told me. Emily has not been blighted with breasts. My sister has a simple elegant swelling that just helps to accentuate her slender waist. My sister has no overhang. Our grandmother has kept my sister's training bra for me to wear and I am wearing it, but my swellings are too big already and the hideous rolls of flesh spill out the side. *Fat girls get titties,* her awful word so terribly appropriate. My fat-girl titties are hidden only by my T-shirt, which I bunch up over them as the invisible wall between her side of the room and mine tumbles down.

'Don't put that shirt on.'

'Why? Why not?'

I turn. The wall is down and I must face her. She is staring straight at me but her head is cocked to one side as if she is listening to someone, an invisible person in the doorway to our room.

'You have to put your shirt on inside out and back to front.'

'Why? No.' I turn away and struggle with the armholes, holding the cotton close and attempting to put my arms in at the same time.

'No!'

She crosses the line. She is on my side of the room, kicking through the detritus on the floor, wading out into the unknown. She launches herself at me as if there were a bomb and I were about to stumble over it. Our lives apparently depend on this business with the T-shirt. She grabs it, and we struggle briefly before she rips it out of my hands and I am left with only my arms to press against the embarrassment of my flesh.

She takes the shirt and turns it, inside out, back to front. She grabs me by one arm and I struggle, but she is stronger. I feel the prick of tears, hot in the corners of my eyes. I am worried that she will look at my breasts but she ignores them. She forces my hand into the shirt and drags it over my head with such force that my ear bends back, caught up in the folds of the fabric. I shriek but she ignores me. Her nails dig into my wrist, the other wrist and it is done. My shirt is on, inside out and back to front. She loses interest instantly. She turns and picks her way over the debris on the floor on my side of the room.

'You should clean your room,' she tells me.

I swipe at my damp eyes with my forearm.

'I am going to turn it round the right way.' I hold the edges of the T-shirt gingerly, lift it slightly and she shrugs. 'I will. I'll do it.'

'Fine.'

'So why did you want me to put it on like this?'

'To save you.' She picks up a jar of blue water, a paintbrush sticking out of it. The only sign that she has been working. Her side of the room is, of course, immaculate.

'What do you mean?'

'It's okay now,' she says, 'do what you like. The danger's gone.'

She lets the door slam closed behind her. I am alone. My eyes still sting. My hair is a tangled mess where she caught it in the neck of my shirt. I struggle to turn the T-shirt and I reach for a cardigan to hide behind.

And then there is this.

Emily stands suddenly and jogs on the spot. She opens the door and runs down the stairs and off towards the fence. It seems she might be about to leave the property. She will be punished for this. We will both be punished. I hurry out to the veranda. She tags the fence as if this were a game. She runs back towards me and I cower to one side, her hand stretched out to hit me, not to hit me, to tap the front door and then she turns again and runs, faster now, panting, sweating, running as if she is being chased. Fence, tap, door, tap, fence, tap, door, tap and I count a dozen repetitions before she stops suddenly and bends over, clutching her knees, catching her breath.

It is a long time before she straightens and even then she grasps at her side and bends a little to ease the pain of a stitch. She slinks past me without even glancing in my direction, but when she opens the door she hisses, 'Don't bother thanking me,' and slams the screen door shut behind her.

And.

She touches a vase sixteen times. Suddenly. Without explanation. Counting.

And.

She turns on her bed and sleeps with her feet touching the headboard.

And.

She crouches in the prickly grass and whispers something to no one and then kills a meat ant with her thumb. I watch her lick it off her finger and swallow it, eyes squeezed tight shut, a grim frown tugging her lips down. She speaks to herself but when I approach she stops and pretends she was not speaking at all.

And one time she pinches me. I am doing nothing. I am sitting in the grass following an ant as it braves a miniature world of struggle and danger, dragging a twig, of all things. It walks backwards, hauling the thing clutched between two strong mandibles. I hold my breath as it reaches a rock and feels for a foothold with one of its back legs. Precarious, life and death, one false move and it will tumble. The stick will crash onto it, the ant will be crushed. Her fingers pinch my arm so hard that my eyes water. Palomino, who is sleeping calmly behind me, his warm dog-scented flank pressed against my back, startles at the sudden movement and scrambles to his feet.

'What?'

But she has turned and is running as if she is frightened that I might chase after her. I rub my arm, which is already starting to bruise. Palomino trails behind me as I walk back to the house. Our mother is standing by the window as if she was watching this exchange. Before our mother snapped she was tightly wound: a leprechaun, our grandmother called her, an imp, a spriggan. A troublemaker, but she says this in a way that makes the word into a compliment. You are just like your mother, she says to Emily sometimes but this is not a compliment.

I let the door swing shut behind me and stand at the window beside my mother and slip my fingers into her hand. Maybe she can feel me. She rarely flinches when I touch her. My voice can't disturb her waking sleep. Only our grandmother can make her sit or stand or eat.

There is still an hour of free play left. Outside my sister stands at the fence line, leaning forward, making the taut wire stretch. I wonder what it looks like to be wound so tight that you might snap. I wonder if our mother used to pinch people all of a sudden or run laps of the garden as if her life depended on it, speak to herself quietly when no one else was there to hear. I imagine Emily after she has snapped: standing at the fence. She wouldn't look any different. She is swinging back and forth and sometimes our mother rocks in her chair. Maybe Emily has snapped already. I watch her until my legs ache from standing too long in the same position. She has grown taller. She looks more like a woman than a child. She is beautiful and slender and yet her waist nips in, giving her an hourglass silhouette.

There is a dark bruise on my upper arm. I wriggle my fingers out of my mother's hand and rub at it. Mother keeps her hand curled over as if my fingers were still in her grasp. I watch as my sister picks one foot up, delicately as a foal, and stretches it through the fencing wire. She points her toe and touches the ground outside our property, turns to look back at the house. She isn't to know that our grandmother is not watching, that the only ones watching are me and our mother, and our mother doesn't notice her at all.

And she picks up the phone again and listens and I know that it is just a part of this madness that is taking her away from me, but I watch her nodding into the handset and I wonder what would happen if I could hear it too. Whoever is on the other end of the phone is there with her now and I am here alone. If only I could see whatever it is that she sees. If only she would let me hear the voice on the other end of the phone. I am frightened but more lonely, perhaps, than scared. I follow her through a world of invisible hurdles, cantering just a little way behind.

Waking Up with Him

He has curled himself into a little ball, pushing his bottom into the curve of my hip. I can feel the heat come off him. He feels too hot, fevered, but this is how he is different from me I suppose. All my limbs are cold, the tips of my breasts are cold. I touch them and they are chilled, the little hard nipples like fingers of ice. He has shuffled so far over to my side of the bed that I can feel the hard edge of the mattress under my back. I suppose he has followed me as I shifted further and further away. I am unused to sleeping with company.

He is like a wombat. This is what strikes me first, how large and round and soft and warm he is, his arms curled up into his chest, his knees butting into his elbows, his nose in his fists. I raise myself gently up onto my elbow to watch him, the beautiful soft expanse of his skin. His back is lightly furred. I remember when Emily and I were lying in the backyard, a conversation about boys. We were teenagers then, a brief interlude where we caught up with each other for a moment. Before this there were years of her racing towards puberty, me lagging, struggling to keep pace.

But on this day we were almost even and she rolled over in the grass. She had taken her top off and laid it on top of her bra, a band of white cotton for modesty, her skin on either side reddened from the sun. I remember watching her pick an ant off her flat stomach and wishing my own stomach were flat like hers. I even wanted her skin, strawberries and cream. My skin was olive and whenever I picked up a drinking glass I smeared oily fingerprints all over it. I kept my shirt on while sunbaking, rested a hat over my face, any scrap of skin exposed to the sun would cook to a deep charcoal colour and Emily would point and tell me I looked like an immigrant, even though I knew Germans are supposed to be pale and not dark at all. I am the colour of my father. This was never mentioned but it was often in the air. I am of my father and therefore lessened.

'When I meet the love of my life he will be smooth. No hair at all on his arms or his chest but messy longish hair on his head. Sandy hair, with white bits like he's been in the ocean. I want him to smell like the sea, and when I put my ear to his chest there will be the sound of the waves.'

This was a good time, before Emily began to leave me. I locked the image of the love of her life into my consciousness, wanting only what she wanted. Slim, hairless, oceanic.

John shifts back towards me a little more, nestling. I lie back on my pillow and put my arms around the hot engine of his body. I rest my cheek on his hairy back and listen. Not the sound of the sea, but the regular thudding of his heart. A live human being, this human being asleep in my bed. I should never have let him stay over. I know this even as I hug him closer, relaxing into the pleasure of this warm body pressed up against mine. I breathe in a great gulp of him and it hits me deep in my gut where I can feel the desire begin. I know I am wet again. Sex on the couch, sex in the bed. He pressed a finger up inside me in the last languid moments before sleep and sighed, pleased to know that if we had the energy I would be ready to join him one more time.

I wriggled down onto his finger, surprised by the little groan that escaped from my lips. 'You should go home,' I told him as he began to move first one finger then two inside me.

'Un huh,' he said, and then, 'there you go,' as he did that thing with his thumb and the contractions started deep inside, curling me back, my head stretched up and around like a new leaf opening to the sun.

It is the smell of him that works its chemical magic on me. I press my face into the furred skin and breathe it. The joy of his warmth and his smell and his big solid body. I suck it all greedily into my memory. I should not have let him sleep over. Maybe I will never let him sleep over again. I let myself soak up all the pure, immediate pleasure. Every good moment must end. This is one thing I have learned in life, chasing after the retreating back of my sister, racing away from me and heading off to some place else.

The Arrival

'He's here.'

Emily sits with her face pressed to the glass. It is raining. Outside the sun is setting, stripping the pale golden glow from the tops of the trees. She holds one hand up to the glass door and her fingers are red as if she has plunged her hand into some-one's chest and torn their heart out. I know it is just paint but there has been something up with her all day. In home-school she was sullen and silent, replying to Oma's philosophical question of the day with barely a shrug. Even at the ritual of feeding Flame, she peered out at the heavy skies instead of checking her steps, so that she tripped over a hidden stone and swore under her breath.

I have been watching her for an hour, glancing up from the novel I am reading to see her frozen, her nose pressed to the glass, red fingers splayed. She looks like a wild cat tensed for the kill. When she speaks I bite my lip, afraid she might pounce on me if I so much as breathe.

I watch her ease back from the window and nod, satisfied. Her hand leaves a smudged print, ghost-fingers. She seems to shrink back into herself as all the pent-up anticipation drains out of her. Emily sinks back onto her heels and whispers.

'Raphael's here.'

I don't know who Raphael is. There is only Emily, Oma, Mother and me. That accounts for all the people in our universe.

Oma is in the kitchen, clattering. Mother sits staring at the blank face of the television. I watch as she turns her head slowly, stares out beyond the greasy prints of my sister's hands, and all the hairs on my neck tug up to attention as a wave of unease trickles cold down my back.

'Stop it,' I whisper to Emily. 'You're scaring me.'

She turns, looking slightly startled as if she had forgotten I was here at all. She stands and walks towards me and I try to hold very still but it is impossible not to flinch when she leaps towards me with her bloody fingers hooked like claws.

'Boo!' she says, then turns and slouches out of the lounge room.

Our mother is still staring out of the window. I clamber up to stand beside her. Outside the darkness is filling in the shadows. There is a rustling and a thumping somewhere out among the trees where, despite the rain, a kangaroo is darting in and out of the dense scrap of bush. Wallabies and paddymelons are making their way across the train tracks and out to the stretches of clear-felled land. Possums uncurl from their damp tree-top beds. Outside the world is waking while inside we are readying ourselves for sleep.

I peer out into the darkness. I know there is no one out there and yet every rustling branch seems like it might have been disturbed by a human hand.

Raphael's here.

She said it just to scare me. And of course it has worked. I stare out of the window for a long time. I hear the hiss of onions hitting hot oil, smell the wonderful rich redness of dinner being prepared. I stare until the darkness steals the edges of the trees, making them shadows among shadows, and still the hairs all stand to attention on my neck. At some point I flinch as my mother suddenly turns back to stare at the television, as if whatever was outside has moved on.

'He's gone now.' The words are past my lips before I can stop them. When I turn around Emily is there behind me. She must have crept back into the room without me noticing. She shakes her head and I feel suddenly ashamed.

Emily goes to set the table and I help her. This is our job. We take our own places and wait for Oma to arrive with the bowl of food.

Emily stares at me unblinking. Just as I am about to ask her who she was talking about, she picks up her knife and grips it with her fist, the tip pointing menacingly down towards the placemat.

'Did you see anything?' she asks, then answers herself with a sly smile. 'Of course not. You didn't see him at all.'

Mother pulls the chair out and sits at the table with us. This is rare, but not completely unheard of. Sometimes her world and ours intersect by sheer luck. Mostly it is Oma's job to lead her here and when she joins us she is confused, staring from one daughter to the other as if wondering who we might be. Today she just sits, resting her fingers lightly on her knife and fork, looking down at her placemat. When our grandmother brings the bowl and ladles pasta and sauce onto her plate she continues to stare until Oma lifts her elbow and directs her fork. I watch as she twirls it in the pasta. She chews, smiling vaguely, swallows. I serve myself. Plenty of garlic today, which is how I like it.

A thump and a rustle. I glance out of the window. Wallabies. Only wallabies, but when I look back towards Emily, she grins knowingly. I stare hard into my bowl, ignoring the prickle on my neck, ignoring the rustle and thump, and continue to eat until my plate is empty.

Stretching

One more canvas. John is here to help but he is less than helpful. It is important that the canvas is stretched as tight as possible and John is young and big with it, although most of his bulk is free from muscle, but he is erratic in his efforts.

He starts the project with his usual jovial enthusiasm.

'I work on paper mostly, or pre-stretched canvases when I'm painting.'

'Stretching is part of the art,' I tell him but I am not sure he believes me. I assumed that a boy would have stronger hands than mine but his hands are small for such a large person. Strange that I have never noticed this. I have noticed the way he uses them, the gentleness, hands like a girl, soft and often smelling like soap. He is a hand washer. This is something else I have noticed. Now I see how the stretcher looks too big for him. He is awkward with it. He fumbles with the handle, strains with the heft of it. I hold the frame in one hand and the staple gun in the other and watch him juggle the one tool awkwardly. His fingers slip on the thick fabric. One section is nicely taut, another too loose. There is a wave in the canvas that is visible without holding the thing up to the light.

'What's wrong with the pre-stretched ones?'

'Not tight enough. They use inferior wood. The finish is not as I want it. The canvas is not the best quality.'

'But the expensive ones. Surely you could just get some expensive ones.'

'To get the quality I want I would have to spend more than I have. We'll just unpick this one and start again.'

'Yes, I suppose so.' But he looks unhappy with this decision. He watches me use the flat edge of a screwdriver to lever the staples out of the wood; his look might just be a glare. He turns, bored with the idea of frames and canvases, and picks up the palette. Bright patches of oil paint with a thin crust setting over it. He sniffs at it.

'Your sister uses acrylics.'

'Sometimes. When we were young it was always oils.'

The canvas slips in my fingers. I clamp it with the metal teeth of the stretcher and lean my whole weight against it. The wooden frame creaks a little. This is the kind of stretch you need. This. Here. Not the inconsistent almost-stretch of John's attempt. I am tempted to get him to come over and look at the tension in the fabric, but he has moved over to the little cluster of my sister's childhood artworks.

'Are you tempted to sell them?'

'No.'

'But imagine how much they're worth.'

'Value.'

'Yeah,' he says, 'value. Is your emotional attachment worth more than half a million dollars, say?'

'I wouldn't get half a million for them.'

'One of your sister's paintings sold for half a million at Sotheby's a couple of weeks ago.'

'Seriously?'

'Don't you Google her?'

'No.'

'You have how many paintings?'

'I don't know, I haven't counted.'

'Do you want me to count?'

'Not particularly. I want you to hold the canvas while I stretch it.'

'But you could get a new car,' he says, ignoring my struggles with the stretcher and the frame.

'I don't need a new car. I like my car.' Two lies, back to back, but he has annoyed me. I pull with all my strength, struggle to hold the stretch and move the staple gun into position at the same time. It is impossible.

'I'm surprised no one has broken into your office and stolen the ones in there. Only now when that happens you'll think it was me and you'll come search my flat.'

'Are you here to help me or what?'

'Sure.'

It is easier with him holding the thing. I finish the first canvas, set it aside, pick up another frame and staple the canvas to one side.

'Are you excited about the exhibition?'

I pause, wipe hair away from my face.

'I'm excited,' he says. 'I love the ones you've finished.'

'They're okay.'

'No,' he says and he seems serious, although sometimes it is hard to tell when he is teasing me. 'They are really great. I'm going to get a suit.'

'What?'

'To wear.'

'Why would you do that?'

'If I'm going to be your handbag I better wear a suit, right?'

I put the stretcher down. It clatters onto the bench, a heavy metal thump and I stretch my fingers out from a cramp.

'You can't be my *handbag*.'

He looks hurt, is suddenly silent. His big dark eyes are hangdog wide.

'We can't be seen together.'

'I'm coming to the exhibition.'

'Sure, but you'll have to go alone, or bring someone else.'

'I don't want to bring someone else. I'm with you.'

'John, do you even listen to me?'

He purses his full lips. It looks odd on him, this pout. His forehead creases with concern. It looks for a moment as if he is about to cry.

'You know sometimes I think you're embarrassed of me. Because I'm not super attractive or because I'm too young or something.'

'You can't be with me, John. You are my student.'

'You always use my name when you are angry with me. Have you noticed that? When you're happy with me you don't call me anything at all.'

'Are you going to help me stretch these canvases?'

He looks at the equipment laid out in front of him. 'No. I don't think I am actually.'

He puts the canvas down and walks out of the studio.

There are canvases leaning against the wall, canvases on the easels, half-finished. There is so much for me to do and it would be easier if he helped me.

'I'm going to put the tea on.'

He is moping on the couch. The scene of our many misdemeanours. When I stand in front of him he looks away.

'John.'

He doesn't even flinch.

'John?'

Nothing.

I sink into the soft leather beside him.

'You are amazing. I really like being around you. But it is completely unethical. You are my student.'

'Loads of people sleep with their students. It happens all the time, it's almost like part of the job description.'

'Not my job description. I am going to have to mark you, you know. How do you expect me to do that now?'

'Fairly? Well? Because I am pretty good at art?'

'Yeah. You are pretty good at art.'

He puts a finger out and touches my hand, strokes the harsh skin there, the pale blue stain where the paint has marked me with its vague tattoo. It is nice to be stroked like this. It is nice to have someone to touch your skin.

'So I'll put the jug on?'

'And I'll get a suit to come to your opening?'

I close my eyes. Shake my head. I feel the weight of him shift on the couch. He is gone and it is cold where his knee was touching mine. The back of my hand tingles. We haven't made love. For some reason I feel terribly betrayed by this fact. The day is ruined. The canvases are unstretched, my mouth is unkissed, my body is ready to be touched and he is leaving.

'You're leaving?'

'I suppose.'

'Okay then,' I say.

And he says, 'Okay.'

I put the jug on anyway. I make tea but I don't want to drink it. I want him to come back. He is my student but I want him to undo the buttons on my shirt, fumble awkwardly with the clasp on my bra. I want to teach him how to unclip me without looking. I wonder if these are maternal feelings, if I am having some weird misplaced mid-life maternal instinct. He is nice this boy, he is good company. When I look at his paintings I feel the lazy places in my head opening, letting new ideas in. He has, in this way, awakened me. My body too. He has made my body hungry for touch again.

I lie awake some nights and think of him the way I used to lie awake and remember the rush of air as I kicked Flame to a gallop. Sometimes with this boy I am fifteen again. That year, and all the things that happened in it. I tip the hot tea down the sink. I couldn't drink it now. I feel nauseous. I should have taken the week off, two weeks, a month. Maybe I should go to China, I have never been able to afford an overseas holiday. I could see my sister again after all these years.

I sit on the couch and stare up at her paintings, counting. Seventeen, and more sketches at the office. I stop myself from counting how much money that would be if each one was valued as much as that one that sold at Sotheby's. Original Early Emily Reichs. Emily Reich. I press my fingers against my eyes and there is some relief from the pain that is building there.

Telephone Reprise

I pick up the telephone. I put it to my ear. I remember the first time I heard him, the sound of breathing in between the flat tones, two conflicting messages. No one is there, someone is there.

Since Emily first started listening to the phone I have snuck in to listen. Now I can hear it every time, his breathing. Why would he be waiting for me to pick up the phone, sitting there, breathing and listening to nothing?

I check to see that there is no one around. I never listen for him when someone is around. The room is empty. We are alone when I say his name.

'Raphael?' because of course it is Raphael. Emily has given me a name for him now. He belongs to Emily, he is her secret, but there is a delicious thrill in stealing this small part of her secret for myself. 'Is that you Raphael?'

Nothing but his breath. No word.

'Don't be afraid, Raphael. I am Emily's sister, Bec.'

Breathing. Beeping. Breathing.

'You could visit me. Just like with Emily. You could visit.'

I look at the fingers of my free hand and they are shaking. I realise now that the chill on my shoulders is not the cold at all. I am frightened. If he were to speak I might scream. I put the phone down quickly and step away from it but the sound of his breathing stays with me.

Exhibit A

He will be here. I step into the gallery and there are any number of reasons to be nervous. I haven't exhibited in years and even though this is a group show there will be people here who I would rather like to impress. My colleagues for one thing, but more importantly the friends of Nancy Gato. Nancy is quite famous. Not as famous as my sister, but enough of a name to drag a handful of journalists out to this stuffy cheese and chardonnay do.

Nancy usually exhibits in vacant lots, laundromats, car parks. She got the idea from the young folk, people the age of my students, John's age. There's a group of them who lug their instruments to late-night public spaces and stage makeshift concerts without permission. The kids think it is awesome, and it is. I would like nothing more than to copy them, set up my canvases balanced on warm throbbing dryers, serve wine in plastic cups out of a cask. John told me about them weeks before Nancy started doing it, and I was tempted to appropriate the idea, shying away because it is not original, frightened that I would be accused of playing catch-up.

I heard about Nancy's show on the afternoon it happened. It was held in a laundromat, exactly like the collective of bands. I bit the inside of my mouth so hard that an ulcer developed in the next few days and I had to gargle with salt water and eat fresh lemons to get rid of it. I felt the regret surge through me like a blush. If I had acted on instinct I would have been there first. It is too late now. Now it is her thing, an exhibition in a pool hall, in a toilet block in an inner-city park, in an alley behind a left-wing bookstore.

I notice Nancy in the far corner of the room surrounded by well-dressed folk, some of them my own students, hovering at a little distance. The photographer snaps away in her direction and Nancy acts bored. Fifty percent of the proceeds will be donated to a soup kitchen to feed the homeless. The waiters are serving little cups of hot soup on silver trays beside rows of sparkling wine.

I pick up a glass of bubbly, drain it and follow the waiter halfway across the room to exchange my empty glass for a full one. I am really very nervous and I have every reason to be, but I am blaming John for my agitation even as I scan the room and find myself disappointed by his absence.

My paintings are on the far right wall between Nancy's flower sculptures and the pointillist works made by the computer programmer guy. I can't remember his name but I remember the process he uses, printing html code onto canvas using coloured numbers. The artist is a game developer and the code is taken directly from his computer game Highschool Sweetheart, set in a public school. Teenagers in a visual art class are given shots of alcohol and encouraged to remove their clothing. Each level of the game is played with younger and younger children until the highest scoring players leave the high school entirely and move to the primary school next door. The code is printed on a huge board and if you stand far enough away from it you can make out a pre-pubescent girl with her legs spread graphically wide.

The room is too small to view this clearly and as more people arrive I watch them standing pressed against the wall near the exit, stretching up onto their toes and craning to see the work over the throng of soup-swilling, champagne-sipping arty types. There are three computers set up in front of the work and a group of students lean towards the screens, playing Highschool Sweetheart, shaking their heads in mock horror as they progress through the various levels, inching towards the primary schoolers with a giggly mix of horror and excitement.

My paintings seem pedestrian in comparison. I was proud of these canvases in the privacy of my own home. I like the way I have managed to capture the light. Each canvas has a face on it, partially out of frame. The skin looks waxy but real. The expressions are open to interpretation. Excitement might be fear, a grin might be a grimace. *Is it ever truly possible to know what someone else is feeling?* I have asked in the required explanation that is typed on a card beside the work. Nancy has written a page of information beside each of her bunches of flowers. There is a book, a mini-thesis to explain the concept behind Highschool Sweetheart. The information is printed on old-fashioned computer paper, the kind we used to use in dot-matrix printers. I watch as people with champagne in one hand unfold page after page, looking for a break in the text before tearing along the perforation.

...*last true sexual taboo*, I hear someone saying as I brush past them...*Brave or crazy*...Another fragment. I have a sense that after tonight the games developer will be more famous than Nancy Gato, although still not as famous as my sister.

Two young women stand in front of my work, staring. I feel suddenly exposed. I take another sip of champagne.

...*more traditional*, I hear one of them say...*engage with trends* and then *old style*.

Old. I hurry away from my portraits, searching desperately for the waiter with the drinks.

There are so many of my students in the crowd and yet John is not among them. I notice one of the girls peering at the printed card beside my work. Is it ever truly possible to read someone else's emotional state? I wonder how the girl is responding to the work; what her own emotional state might be, but when I glance in her direction she just seems terribly bored. I know how lame my explanation sounds. I know that my work is not nearly as conceptually complex as the rest of it. For some crazy reason I imagined this to be a strength: the art stands for itself. It is not about anything that you can't see from looking at the work.

When they bring us up to the microphone it feels like a cattle call. I am the most awkward artist in the room. I am not as casually ruffled as the others. My dress is old but not as old-made-fashionable as Nancy's fifties frock. The programmer, whose name is Duane, is wearing a hoodie under his suit jacket as all good programmers must. There is an Egyptian artist who speaks very little English and who is therefore not required to make any kind of speech at all. The fifth artist is at a show in Germany and sends his apologies.

I try to listen to what Nancy Gato is saying, something about site-specific work and the ephemeral nature of aesthetics. At least I try to look as if I am listening. John slips into the room just as the founder of the soup kitchen is asking Nancy about her work and its relationship to the disenfranchised.

John seems a little awkward from this distance. He is slightly pigeon-toed and it gives his walk a strange unbalanced edge. He seems to rock from foot to foot as he moves through the crowd. I have to stop myself from waving. I have had several glasses of champagne and it is easy in this state to imagine that he is my actual partner, someone I love, who is here to support me. He ducks his head so as not to meet my gaze. One of the students I recognise waves to him and he moves gratefully to stand with her group. They laugh, all of them, and for a moment I imagine that they are all laughing at me but of course they're not. Nancy has said something amusing. I smile, a slightly delayed response and then everyone is clapping, whispering to each other.

I hear my name and must seem startled as I look towards the founder of the soup kitchen, a young and stylish woman, surprisingly good looking, with an expensive asymmetrical haircut and a large wide mouth that stretches back to reveal perfect teeth.

'Feelings?' she asks and I feel sweat spring up on my palms, my own unambiguous emotional response.

'I have a theory that if you are too close to someone it's impossible to see them objectively. Their emotions become reflections of your own emotions. There is no distance. That's what I've done with the work, removed the distance, physically. Actually I haven't written much of an explanation for it because sometimes the images have to stand for themselves. There isn't really anything more than that. What they are, here, physically in the space.'

She nods. I have left her no room for another question and I feel suddenly guilty about this.

'But it is physical, you know. Painting, for me. It is about the oil and the pigment on the canvas. It is kind of like—something—swimming—or—dancing—or something.'

I wince. I can't believe I have said all of that. Some of my students are in the room. John is here, looking helplessly towards me.

'It's a completely different process for me than, say, what Duane does.' I turn to Duane. I direct the attention away from me and towards Duane. The founder of the soup kitchen asks Duane if art is a physical exercise for him, and of course it is not. He is well versed in the theory behind his images. He explains his thesis about taboos. The act of making the viewer an ethical reader of the work. Making their participation both pleasurable and uncomfortable. At the end of his talk the audience clap and cheer. It is only afterwards, stepping out of the line, that I realise there was never an opportunity for people to clap for me.

He is here in the crowd somewhere and I could find him, stand with him. He is my student and therefore I have a reason to be speaking with him. We could be discussing art. I find another waiter and relieve him of yet another glass of champagne. Maybe I can leave after this glass. No one will notice. They are too busy trying to speak to Duane. I turn and there is Nancy Gato and because we are standing so close she must acknowledge me.

'Hi,' she says, and, 'well done, with…' She gestures vaguely in the direction of our paintings, pointing directly at Duane's computer terminals but she is not really looking so she is not to know.

'Yes. Good work with the flowers.'

'Well they're not actually flowers, which is the point, but I know what you mean and thank you.'

I turn to look at her bunches of flowers which really do look like flowers and wish I had taken a moment to read the program before being forced into a conversation with Nancy Gato.

'Your work is much less aggressive than your sister's isn't it?' she says and I shrug.

'That's one way of putting it.'

'Well Emily's work is so—passionate.'

By which she means my work is cold. It was a word used in one of the brief reviews of my first exhibition, *cold, reserved*, and the words have haunted me ever since.

'Yes. But I am not mentally ill,' I tell her and I can hear the champagne bubbling up into my conversation. I try to rein it in but it is too late now. 'I think that has an impact on my work.'

'Not that all artists have to be mad.'

'No, no, of course not. But it certainly helps, don't you think?'

Nancy giggles nervously and eases herself back just a little as I forge ahead. 'The visions I mean, the hallucinations. But I suppose we could just take drugs.'

'Or drink too much.'

'Mmm.' I nod. Take another gulp of champagne. 'Well, cheers to you.'

'And to you.'

We clink glasses and the gesture releases her to move on to other, less drunk, conversations. I swear under my breath. I look towards the door, make my way in that direction. There is nowhere to put my glass. Why don't they put tables out at these things for the empty glasses?

I feel a hand on my elbow and swing around too quickly. John laughs. I have spilled his champagne.

'I thought you were trying to escape,' he says.

'I was.'

'Well don't. I want you to meet my friend.'

I notice her now. A pretty girl, short dark bob. A little black dress worn a bit self-consciously. Too much makeup. I try to smile, but I know it looks more like a grimace. It is too late for me to save this.

'Hi.' I extend my hand. 'Bec,' I tell her and she shakes my hand, a frightened little brush of her limp fingers.

'Bec, this is Lindsay. Lindsay this is Bec.'

'Hi.'

'I just hate these things, don't you?'

'Yes,' she grins, grateful. 'I never know what to do with my hands.'

Her arms are folded, her hands tucked under her neat little breasts. She seems so young and I have to remind myself that she is John's age. John is so young too. John is my student and the fact that he is also my lover is something that no one else knows. I wonder if she noticed how familiar I was with John before I realised she was there behind him. I wonder if she has guessed that he is more than just a student of mine.

'Bec is Emily Reich's sister.'

She drops her hands suddenly to her sides. I notice the twitch in her fingers. Her eyes widen slightly and she presses her lips together as if she wishes she had not said anything to me at all.

'You know Emily's work, right?'

She nods slowly. Of course she knows my sister's work. People who have never seen an original work of art, people who decorate their walls with prints from a homewares store have heard of Emily Reich. She reaches for John's elbow and holds it firmly between her thin birdlike fingers, as if the solidity could protect her from this unexpected brush with fame.

'Lindsay goes to TAFE at the moment,' he explains to me, 'but she's going to come over to the university next year. Aren't you Lindsay?'

The small girl nods, looks down at her shoes, which are too high and too shiny, straight out of the box. She holds John's elbow between both of her tiny hands and he pats her fingers paternally.

'I was just…' I indicate the door.

'Oh. I have some more friends who'd like to meet you if you have a minute.'

'I really have to…'

'Oh. Okay. Well. Good show. With the work and everything. See you in class?'

'Yes.'

When I am out on the footpath I realise that I am still carrying the champagne glass. I shake it and slip it into my handbag.

Raphael

The summer I turn fifteen, I stand by uselessly as the madness takes her. 'Takes' is the right word. All our hard-earned intimacy is stripped away. She whispers to herself when before she might have whispered to me. She plays games with the wind and the sky and the tall grasses by the gate but when I try to drag her to play one of our own games she stands and stares as if the real world is just an echo of something, a trick of the light. She gazes through me, smiles, then turns and walks away.

When the madness took her is the way Oma has always put it, resting her hand lightly on our mother's shoulder. I watch Emily strolling away from me, angling her head as if she is listening to someone beside her, and I know what Oma means by *taken*.

I do not want to be left alone like this. Emily picks up the phone and holds it to her ear and nods. When she places it back in the cradle I am there beside her. I will not be left out of this change in her life. She eases out of the lounge chair and I settle into the warm hug, the scent of her lavender on the scratchy fabric. I pick up the phone, hold it to my ear. She is watching me closely, perching on the lounge chair opposite, tucking her feet up underneath her. Her gaze is steady and unwavering. I hold the phone hard against my ear and breathe in. The smell of her breath on the mouthpiece, the sticky slip of her fingerprints against mine.

'Hello?'

If I listen very closely there is the sound of breathing. My breathing perhaps, reflected back to me, but I want it to be his breath. I want to share him with her. Raphael has stolen my sister from me and I want so much to join them in their game.

She is watching with her large dark eyes. I know that mine are pale and furtive in comparison. For now, just this moment, I have her complete attention.

'Hello?' I whisper into the handset. My fingers are trembling. I can hear the breathing, my own or someone else's, but it is loud and fast, scrappy breaths as if whoever it is has been running or is perhaps afraid.

'Is anyone there?'

I close my eyes but she is still watching me. I can feel it. My head throbs. A nerve in my temple starts to twitch.

Please, please please please answer the phone. Answer the phone.

If you don't answer she will be lost to me. You will have her all to yourself.

I hear a catch in my breath, a sob. I bite my lip, open my eyes. I think I might cry. I sniff. Don't let her see you cry. My lip is trembling and the more I try to stop it, the larger the twitching seems.

The voice is far off. It is like static. It is almost not a voice at all, it is the hiss of fibres rattling soundwaves from one place to another, the clicking of electric signals, but when I strain to make sense of the hiss there are words in it.

'Can you hear me?' My eyes widen, my hands are clammy on the phone.

'Yes,' I say, 'yes I can hear you.'

'You can hear me?'

'Yes.'

'You can hear me?'

'Yes.'

I look up. Emily is staring at me. It is as if she is seeing me for the first time in months. There is a look on her face, relief perhaps, a relaxing of the muscles around her mouth. She smiles and it is a genuine smile.

I can hear him. She knows I can hear him. It is as if his voice, tiny and muffled, hidden in a thick fog, is a ladder between her world and mine. I cling to the rung I am holding with everything I have. My knuckles are pale and tight, my fingers ache.

I hunt for the staticky words and find them. 'Is this you?'

He says, 'Yes.'

'I am Emily's sister.'

'Pleased to meet you,' says Raphael.

Paintings

Paintings by Emily Reich. When I open my eyes they are all there lined up on the wall. John could bring his little friend around for a tour. I am rich. Under the painting of the burning cow my shoes lie scuffed and cheap and worn at the heel. My dress is a fallen thing beside them, fading slightly, the hem frayed. A small hole burnt into the skirt provides a peep show of the floorboards below. My car door does not close properly and the interior light runs the battery down unless I am vigilant. The pilot light in the gas heating is erratic. Yet here I am, rich beyond my wildest dreams if you count my sister's work as currency.

John reached out a finger the first time he was here, naked, all the awkwardness of consummation behind us. He stood with the comfortable overhang of his belly shading a shrivelled penis. Little snail, I thought, and watched him stretch out that one finger and touch the thick paint on the surface of the canvas. Like he was touching god. He seemed frightened, as if an alarm might suddenly trip and catch him here despoiling a national treasure.

I am drunk. My face is numb. My hand is almost a blur in front of my eyes. I touch my cheek with clumsy fingers. A hot wave of liquid rushes up my oesophagus. I sit up and it retreats. I must not lie down. We lay down on this couch, John and I. I stand and move towards her paintings. I reach with my own finger and touch the surface. I watched Emily applying the paint, meticulous, using a brush with a single hair of sable for the very fine details, the lashes, the flare in the eye, the large pores at the side of the nose, the fine hairs spilling over the hooves.

I take the stairs slowly, I am unsteady even without my high heels. The floor of the studio is cold and I wish now I had changed into some slippers. The spilt paint spikes up into the tender underside of my toes. There are paintings half-finished, leaning against the walls. A large close-up of an eye, part of an ear, the edge of a mouth, lips slightly parted as if to kiss or to shriek. It would have made it into the exhibition, this large work, if I had had two more days, three at the most. Maybe this one painting would have changed the whole thing, made everything better. Maybe if this canvas were hanging in the gallery now, John would be here beside me.

I wear the key around my neck at all times. It is old and looks decorative. I like the shape and weight of it.

What does that open?

I remember him picking it up off my chest, the end of it grazing against my nipple. I remember him kissing the flesh there as if in apology, the kiss opening to the wetness of his tongue, the pleasure of my skin entering his mouth.

My heart, I told him, and he pressed his hand against mine which was wildly beating in my chest.

Then you should give it to me.

If you want my heart you will have to work for it.

I pull the key up and over my head. It sits in the palm of my hand, heavy as history.

The paintings are a solid weight against my thighs but I am used to the lean of them settling into my lap. Behind them there is a small door, a low cupboard, a lock. I fit the key into it and turn it.

Bluebeard kept the bodies of the women he had killed: I remember the terrible heart of his story. When our Oma told us his secret, Emily's eyes gleamed but I was scared witless.

Here is my terrible heart. I pull the canvases out one by one. I study the colour and shape, the technique. I hold up a canvas that is almost an Emily Reich. I know how to make the light come from one direction, head on, giving a startling starkness to the figure there. I know how to make the feathers slip over into flesh, the arms disappearing into fur, the wool morphing into the curls on a baby's head. I know how she does it because I have spent hours watching her do it, hours doing it myself. Like an insect hiding itself in the form of a leaf, my paintings are almost indistinguishable from the original Emily Reichs upstairs hanging on the wall.

I count these canvases, adding them up in half-million units. A hidden fortune in forgeries, I suppose. I know the signature is perfect. When I was a child she sometimes made me sign her paintings for her and I did it laughing, knowing that it was wrong, insisting she sign my own paintings too. You couldn't tell the difference between Emily's signature and mine. I wonder if that painting at Sotheby's carried my maker's stamp on her work.

I stop at a painting of a man who is a bird, anchored to a branch with a length of razor wire. I don't remember painting this one at all. Perhaps this is an actual Emily Reich, hidden down here with all my fake Emilys by accident.

I pull the painting out and rest it against the wall. Maybe I have just forgotten. I should hang it upstairs with all my sister's true work. I pause just before locking the door, open it, put the painting back into the alcove. There is a chance that it is one of mine after all. I have a vague memory of realising that feathers need a steady hand, making one tiny line overlap another till the lines become feathery. Maybe I painted it early in my Emily Reich period, when it was impossible for me to see where Bec ended and Emily began.

I lock the cupboard and pile my own worthless canvases in front of the door. I hang the key around my neck where it thumps gently against my right breast.

You will have to work to win my heart instead.

That's fair enough. It's okay anyway I am a really hard worker.

The next Emily Reich I paint will have his face and perhaps the body of a bear. I can see it now, an image forming somewhere deep in my subconscious. John as a big warm friendly bear, only I will become Emily in the painting of it and therefore when the bear opens his mouth to take my nipple between his lips we will see the glint of teeth sharp enough to tear flesh and crunch up bones. With my own work the expressions are uncertain. So this, then, is where Bec ends and Emily begins. When I become Emily, my intentions are never ambiguous; they are awfully sharp and horribly clear.

Best Friends

I put down the telephone and Emily opens her wings like a dark angel. I am cradled in the gorgeous threat of her attention once more.

'Did you hear him?'

I nod.

'Did you hear his voice?'

'He was whispering.'

She nods sagely. 'He has to whisper. He is a secret.' She is holding my elbow and her fingers clamp down on the sensitive skin there, pinching it. 'You understand that don't you?'

I nod, but her grip tightens till my eyes start to tear up.

'He is a secret from Oma and everyone. You can't tell Oma. You can't tell anyone about him. Do you understand?'

I nod and she releases me suddenly. There are white marks on my elbow. The blood rushes into them and throbs. I wipe my eyes with the back of my hand.

'I understand,' I say and she nods again.

'He visits me.'

'When?'

'Sometimes. At night.'

I feel the sharp prick of jealousy. My sister, who is all I have in the world, off with her secret friend in the middle of the night.

I want more than anything for him to visit me too. There is a sudden emptiness in the centre of my chest. It must have been there all along but it feels like it has only just opened up.

My sister reaches out and I cinch my elbows close in to my body. She puts her arms around me in a hug. Such a rare gift, I settle into the brief comfort of it.

'You can hear Raphael too.' She hugs me tighter. It is uncomfortable but I cling to her arms and breathe in the lavender of her skin, savouring the brief sweetness of it before she withdraws the warmth of her body.

It is easy to hear his voice now that I know what I am searching for among the hissing. His voice is just a tiny crackle of static turned into words through a huge amount of concentration. I wonder, as I listen, if the furrow that I feel creasing my brow makes me look more like Emily. I certainly hope it does. She looks enigmatic whenever she talks to Raphael, mysterious, a creature from another world. Raphael's world. I feel like an intruder. It takes me minutes sometimes to conjure his voice from the flat beeping of the phone but it gets easier with practice, and every time our Oma locks herself in her study to restore the paintings I pick up the phone. I practise hearing him.

'Emily?' he says.

I smile because just this once he has mistaken me for her, and I hesitate. I do not want to correct him. I want him to say to me whatever he would be planning to say to Emily herself.

'Yes,' I say. 'It's me.'

'Emily.'

I smile when he says her name. Her skin on my shoulders allows me to be confident.

'Yes, Raphael, it's me.'

What would he say to Emily, I wonder. I strain to hear his voice through the dead flat tone of the telephone. What would he tell her?

'Shall I come for you tonight?' That is what he says.

And I say, 'Yes.'

My heart is racing. There is a sheen of sweat on the palms of my hands.

'See you tonight.'

'Okay.' My hand is shaking when I replace the handset.

Emily sees Raphael. She has told me this. An apparition of flesh and blood and breath. Now is my time. It is wonderful but it is terrible as well. Now I will just have to make him real.

Dead White Guys

John is late for class. This is such a rare event that everyone grins and nudges him as he pushes past the rows of desks to find his regular position near the front of the room. He sits and I smile towards him and he looks down at his desk. I notice a blush creeping up and into his cheeks. It is raining outside and his hair is damp and he seems edgier than usual. Something is wrong. He shuffles his books onto the table and barely glances towards the front of the room. I am Emily Reich's sister. That is how he introduced me to his pretty friend last night. The sister of Emily Reich, teaching him art history.

I press the remote and the next slide flashes up onto the screen. A portrait of a dead white guy.

The students are bored. I am bored. We talk about paintings that were made for silent contemplation. *The painting stands for itself.* I shudder. My head is still woolly from too much champagne, my feet still hurt from the shoes I shoved them into. I am Emily Reich's sister and that alone was the reason I was invited to exhibit in the first place. When Emily exhibited in London six years ago she stepped up to the microphone and told the audience to go home. She shouted at them to go away. Go away. Go away. It is exactly what I felt like doing last night. When Emily did it the audience were thrilled. The media was abuzz with the news. Emily Reich Causes Scene in London Art World. Last night I did nothing but bore them all.

I change the slide.

'This,' I say, 'is a dead white guy.'

The flick and flash of the slide changing.

'This is a painting by a dead white guy.'

Next slide.

'Dead white guy.'

'Painting by a dead white guy. Painting. Painting. Dead white guy.'

I press the button faster and faster. The images flick on and off and there is a flare of white light in between. I notice John raise his wide eyes to the screen. I have his attention. He looks frightened. I didn't want to frighten him. The rest of the class are awake now. People shift upright in their chairs. This must be what it feels like for Emily, throwing a tantrum in front of the artful elite. I remember her tantrums. I remember the frightening well of anger so easily tapped. The aftermath.

There is no way I could muster the same kind of hatred and pain. I look at John directly and he looks guilty. I can conjure up the memory of the pretty young girl, the TAFE student and the pride in John's face as he introduced me as Emily's sister. I am certain she was impressed. He knows Emily's sister. He knows her to talk to and to drink with. I wonder if he mentioned that we have been lovers. I am Emily Reich's sister's lover. Was Emily Reich's sister's lover, because it is clear to me that he has another lover now.

He is a boy, my student and so very, very young. I am the responsible adult in this situation. I wonder if it is because of this that I can't quite work up the same kind of anger that my sister could conjure at a whim.

I press the button and the screen reflects my desktop. Folders for my files, folders for home, folders for ideas, a messy pile of files spread out across the screen, none of them snapped to any kind of grid, a whole big compost heap of downloads in the top right corner, file upon file upon file. Emily's voice in my head, *You should tidy your room Rebecca.* I close the laptop and the screen goes blank.

'So anyway if you want to pass your exam then you probably need the information that goes with the images of all those dead white guys, right? So if you want to you can look in your dossier and get the notes I have written for this week's lecture and read them for yourself. You can do this now. You all have your laptops? You can download them from the website. Or else you can go home and do it there. It's raining. The library is dry. Or you can maybe not bother until the night before the exam, which is what you all used to do in high school, right? Didn't seem to do anyone here any harm. You all got into university?'

I pack my computer into my bag and head for the door. They turn to watch me leave like the heads of sunflowers following the light. Yes. This is how you win their love and respect. My sister knew this all along.

I pause at the door and turn and tell them, 'And don't even

think about skipping life drawing class tomorrow. Art history you can learn from a book, but unless you have a model in your own home and put the time aside to draw, I expect to see each and every one of you. On time.'

'Hey.' Ed catches me when I turn the corner and it is a shock to see him. I am suddenly ashamed of my actions. What if one of my students complains to Ed? He is wearing a T-shirt with a square of cartoon panels on it. It would be rude to stare at his shirt, but I wonder what irony is held in the printed squares.

'Did you get the paper?'

'No.' Although of course I usually do.

'You didn't see the review of your exhibition? You should get the paper. Hey, sorry I got there late. I looked for you.'

'Yeah, I left pretty early.'

'You okay?'

I snap my lips shut, look towards the pile of books and notes in my hands.

'You need to take time off, remember?'

'Okay.'

He checks his watch and he is walking backwards, shouting to me even as he disappears back down the corridor, 'Get the paper. Oh, and congrats. The paintings are—' I can't make out the last word. I turn and walk less purposefully toward the exit.

There is a long walk from the classroom to my car. By the end of the corridor I have repented. If John runs to catch me up while I am still in the building then I will take it as a sign that he has only kissed her. I take the stairs one at a time, pausing at each landing. If he used the lift he would certainly overtake me. I pause at the door to the building as long as I am able.

107

Outside on the lawn I decide that if he catches me at my car then maybe they made out a little but did not sleep together. I have not brought an umbrella. I hug my notes to my chest. The laptop is inside its water-resistant sleeve but I am still a little concerned for it as I feel the rivulets of rain cascading down my back.

My shoes take in water and I am suddenly reminded of the boots I used to keep for rainy days, sticking in the mud of our yard, leeches, the smell of clothing that has sat too long on the laundry floor in a puddle of its own making. The year of the flood. My fifteenth year.

I open the door of the car and get in. I sit and drip.

He is younger than me. So much younger. He is my student and what I have done with him is wrong. Still I wait and watch the doorway. Students scurry out, covering their heads with their handbags, slipping folders under their T-shirts. The rain has surprised us all.

I start the engine. Then, eventually, I drive home.

'I don't know what you want me to do.'

He is standing in the rain and there is no point inviting him in now. It is too late, he can't get any wetter. It is a warm rain. He shivers a little but it can't be from cold. I stand in the doorway, blocking any entry he might be hoping to make.

'I feel like everything is a test all the time only I can't win.'

'We can't be together,' I tell him, and he holds his hands out, palms upwards as if to catch great handfuls of rain.

'Yeah. So, I go to a gallery opening with a girl and I get punished for it? You wouldn't go with me.'

'I can't.'

'I know. You knew I wanted to be your date. You told me to ask someone else.'

'Date? You sound like you're fourteen.'

'Well that's what you're acting like.'

'"How you're acting",' I correct him.

'Oh. Right. And pretending you're my mother is a step forward?'

My chest is too tight to breathe. I step back and there is room for him to come inside if he chooses to. He jigs from foot to foot as if he needs to go to the toilet.

'Are we having a fight?' I ask and he lowers his handfuls of water so that they drip onto the ground.

'I suppose so.' He stares down at his wet sandshoes.

'Are you going to come in?'

He looks up at me, his eyes are impossibly large and round. 'I kissed that girl.'

He is lovely. So shy and earnest and the best artist I know, except for my sister of course. There is always my sister.

'She was a bit excited that you knew Emily Reich's sister, wasn't she?'

He steps back. His shoulders look defeated. 'So you want me to come in? Or maybe not.'

'I can't sleep with my students. It's unethical.'

'So you keep saying.'

'See, now it is going to be even more awkward.'

'What? I shouldn't have kissed her?'

'Kissed is a euphemism I assume?'

'What? You want pictures?'

'No,' I say, stepping back to guard the doorway. 'I don't suppose you'll be coming in.'

He stands there with his slump-shoulders and his large intelligent eyes and I close the door and lean my forehead against it and listen to him, standing quietly there in the rain.

There is something ridiculous about how much I want to be hugged by him right now. I suppose he needs a hug too. If there were one of those peep holes in the door I could look through it and watch him standing, soaked and miserable.

I make tea and sit in the lounge room facing my sister's painting. This is what he would have seen, looking up over my shoulder, sliding into me. More flesh on my bones than necessary, a pillow of flesh for him to lean into. I pick up the pile of marking and move over to the other side of the couch. This is where I was sitting that first time. I stretch out my hand, remembering his fingers. The first intimate gesture, the caress of his index finger up and down against mine, the tender curl of his hand, the innocence of such a gesture, the sweetness of our fingers tangling like an ill-fitting jigsaw puzzle. His fingers interlinked with mine. It is impossible not to associate this gesture with Raphael. I feel the hairs begin to rise on my neck.

His assignment is somewhere in this pile. I take the first sheaf of papers off the stack and glance at the name on the second one. This is like a game of Russian roulette. At some point his name will come up and I will be too hard on him, or too easy, depending which swing of the pendulum has come around at the time.

I shuffle pages, tapping the stack of paper against the coffee table, straightening the sheets. There are words but I can't seem to focus on them. I put the essay down and press the palms of my hands into my eyes. Motes of light dance in the darkness, changing colour like a screensaver.

'This is why you don't sleep with your students.'

I can feel the blood pulsing in my temples. When I push the table away the pile of assignments topples, spilling onto the floor. There are still morphine tablets left over from my hospital stint last week. I rummage through the medicine drawer till I find the packet. I take one. It doesn't hurt so much if I bend my head over and onto the cradle of my arms. I sit like this at the kitchen table till the drugs kick in and it feels safe enough to move.

I open the fridge and stare into it as if the various mouldy stubs of carrots and zucchini might hold the answer to my problems.

I shut the fridge and rifle through my backpack. It is impossible to find anything in here. Purse, three books, two sketchpads, pencils, a box of oil pastels, some of them spilt and turning everything else in there to a blue smudge. I take them all out one at a time and pile them on the kitchen bench with the rest of the debris. There at the bottom of it all, among the shattered fragments of a stick of charcoal, is my phone. I shake it and the coarse black powder scatters onto the kitchen bench like dandruff.

It hurts my eyes to focus on the screen. My head is pounding and I am overcome by a wave of nausea as I type. *I think I went back to work too soon.* My fingers become black from the charcoal dust. *I think I need to take some time out. Is there anyone who can do my marking for me?*

I sit with the message reading it over several times before pressing send. It is as if the send button is a detonator. Something explodes in my head and my eyes water with the pain. I feel my way down the corridor and lower myself cautiously onto my unmade bed. Even the cotton pillowcase feels too harsh against my cheek.

I have slept with my student, not just once, not just an awkward mistake, but several times, almost enough to call it a relationship. The sound of the rain smells like rotting flesh. I feel nauseous. Something buzzes like an electric shock in my fist. I wonder if I am still in hospital, if I have been given some kind of shock therapy for my sins, but there in my hand is my phone and the blinding flare of a message on the screen. I peer at it through almost closed lids.

Of course. I'll pick up your assignments tomorrow after work. Take a few weeks off. That is an order. Ed.

I feel like I have lost a battle I didn't realise I was fighting.

There is only one painting in this room, something I did in art school, a young girl caught in the act of turning away from the viewer. It looks like it is painted from a photograph but I did it from reflections in the mirror. One eye visible, partially obscured by hair.

I did have sex with him in this bed but mostly we did it in the lounge room where the traces of my sister are ever-present. I made love to him as he stared up and around with those huge awe-struck eyes, startled to be there in that room surrounded by paintings he recognised from books and magazines. A brush with fame. Having sex with Emily Reich's sister. Excited by the very idea of it.

I close my eyes and drag a pillow up over my head and eventually the nausea passes. Just a migraine. It has been a difficult week. I place my hands on my belly where the five scars are still red and raised, but healing. Something has been taken out of me. Something is missing. He is walking home through the rain or sitting on a bus and I am here holding my tender swollen stomach as if I had just lost a foetus I was carrying.

Meeting Raphael

Emily wakes me. It must be Emily, but I can tell in the darkness that it is not. It is not the way Emily would stand. He stands at a lean. I suppose you would call it a slouch. When he rocks forward a little the light from the window falls on his cheek and I notice the set of his jaw. Not Emily at all.

Raphael is just as I imagined he would be. I look behind him to where my sister's bed is pressed against the wall, the dark bundle of her sleeping body. Maybe I am sleeping too. Maybe this is part of some complicated dream and in a moment the boy standing in front of me will melt away into the darkness like every other shadow.

He is thin. His hair is a sandy thatch, the front of it sticks up and out like the brim of a cap, shading a high forehead and pre-maturely receding hairline. I remember lying in the grass beside Emily. Talking about boys. He is the kind of boy Emily described. Sandy hair, bleached from the ocean. His eyes are deep set and dark and his eyebrows are a little too thick for someone so young, giving him a wise but concerned expression. He might be my own age or older like my sister, but he might be older still, almost an adult. He has one of those faces where it is impossible to tell. He stands with his arms out and his fingers splayed as if to assure me that he has no weapon.

'Raphael.'

Raphael raises a finger and places it against his lips. The house is silent. I can hear a scrambling through tall grass outside which might be a possum or a wallaby, a thump as a cane toad flings itself against the glass of the sliding door. All the sounds safely locked out in the tepid night air.

He nods towards the corridor, a sweet little gesture, a playful bob. He disappears out of the room and I am alone again. I wonder if I am frightened. I certainly notice the racing of my heart. I slide my legs over the side of the bed and onto the debris on the floor, picking my way across the room. There is a dream-like quality to it all. The quiet shuffle of my steps, the silence of the room.

He is standing in the lounge. The windows are all locked. The doors are all locked. There is no way he could have slipped inside without a key, or without breaking something. He can't be real. He is a figment of my sister's imagination and he has somehow slipped out and into my dreams. I am asleep. I am certain this is true and yet I know also that I am wide awake. Raphael steps closer and I recoil as if from a phantom. His fingers brush my hand, curl around to clasp me; he feels real enough. He leads me towards my own front door and I can tell he has been here many times before.

The door is locked. He turns the metal handle and slides the bolt across. I am still slow and fuddled and for a moment I am back in home-school classes. The concept of parasites, invisible things living inside their host undetected. Maybe Raphael lives in the house, somewhere in the walls. If this were an old and crumbling mansion then it might be true, but this is a new building, thin walls, built to a plan. Raphael is here inside a locked house and the only explanation seems to be that I am still sleeping.

He stands in the doorway and tips his head back a little, pointing at me with his chin. It is a small gesture. A normalising little tilt of the head. This is a real live boy, not a dream or a demon or one of my sister's fantasies. Here is a person, standing in my doorway and silently suggesting we step outside.

A wallaby hops away, startled. I step down onto the dry crackle of grass. There is a slight breeze and the shrubs make the best use of it, shivering despite the heat on the wind. It is 2am and the world is still sweating from yesterday.

There is nothing unearthly about him, he is wearing a T-shirt and jeans. His eyes are quite large and very dark but his face is a normal boy-shaped face, a little on the underfed side. He is at that stage where he has grown upward without growing outward.

'Raphael. It is Raphael, isn't it?'

He shrugs. 'I've seen you around,' he says, casually. 'But you are prettier close up. You have a lovely face.'

I feel the heat of blood rushing into my cheeks. I glance up at the sky and there are all the stars, so many of them, an unbroken carpet of stars.

'I thought Emily had invented you.'

He laughs. It is a lovely rolling sound that seems like it will never end, half giggle, half song.

'Seriously. I thought she was making you up. Teasing me. She makes stuff up sometimes. Why haven't I seen you before?'

'And yet I've seen you. And I've heard a lot about you already.'

'We should wake Emily up.'

'Should we?'

I glance back at our window, the dark glass there, the silence behind it. He is real or I am asleep. I have an overpowering urge to touch him. To feel that his skin is warm and alive. If I were to climb back into bed now I would not believe this in the morning.

There is a moon, but it is only a muted glow through a high, fine layering of cloud that now drifts, dreamlike, across the starscape. Sometimes I wake in the night and my sister's bed is empty. Sometimes she is up and pacing in the lounge room. Sometimes she is out in the yard. I have caught glimpses of her behind the curtain, calmer when she is confronted by the open space, acres of ground used for nothing but running cattle. Scrub and high dead grass and anthills the size of bicycles.

One particular night I looked out to see her crouching by the fence with her hands stretched through it, her fingers curling around the sense of freedom that lies outside. The bedroom window was ajar, the cold wind creeping through the chink in the armour of our house. When I pressed my face against the glass and made a shade of my hands I could see that she was speaking, to herself or to someone else. To Raphael, perhaps. Yes; in hindsight it might have been Raphael. There might have been someone standing hidden behind the tree line.

Raphael raises his hand. It would be an easy thing to take it, to feel his fingers in mine, to know he is real with flesh and blood and heat. It would be easy enough. I cross my arms over my chest.

I am wearing a summer nightdress and I am suddenly aware of my chest, the puffiness under the thin cotton. I hunch my shoulders, clutching my ribcage.

'I'm not dressed. I shouldn't be outside.'

'That,' says Raphael, 'is the adventure. Snakes in the grass, dingos hunting, cane toads underfoot. Alive, right?'

'Did Emily give you a key?'

'Emily,' he says then, looking over my shoulder to the window, Emily asleep behind it. 'Do we wake Emily?'

I am outside at night in my nightdress and if my grandmother found me here I cannot bear the thought of what would happen. And what if Emily wakes and finds me outside with her friend? Her Raphael?

'I've got to go back,' I say.

'No.'

'I'll get in trouble. This is awful.'

Talking to a strange boy in the dark, in my nightdress. I take a step back towards the house.

'If you stay with me nothing bad will happen. I promise you.'

Emily's Raphael. Raphael belonging to Emily. My heart is racing now. I inch backwards, keeping an eye on him. If I turn my back on him what might happen?

I turn and run the last few steps up to the veranda, taking several of the concrete stairs at a time and closing the door behind me. I lean on it and slide the bolt across. He was inside. I woke and he was there. Simple as that. My face feels too hot. I put my hand onto my forehead. Maybe I have a fever and Raphael is just an invention of my struggling brain.

I peer through the glass. It is dark outside but I can see him.

Pale, his hair like something shattered and swept into a pile. I watch as he reaches into his jeans pocket and takes something out, a pouch of tobacco. It must be difficult to reach into it and balance the pack, take a paper out and roll, but he does it so smoothly it is like a ballet of his fingers. He puts the pouch away and lights the end of his cigarette, the thing glows then dies then glows again as he sucks on it. He is staring directly at the house, a solid thing, not a figment of some illness.

He points at me. It is dark in the house and I am not sure he can see me standing here, peering through the space where the curtain does not quite meet the wall, but he points in exactly my direction. His lips stretch wide as he mouths, *Come outside*. He can't see me, it is not possible, but I shake my head anyway.

I watch him. He watches me. There is enough light and he is pale. For some reason, when Emily first spoke of him I imagined him dark. Dark haired, olive skinned, a true creature of the night. This boy is so pale I suppose, like Emily, he turns lobster red if he goes out in daylight without sunscreen. I imagine his skin becomes freckled. His hair has that bleached look of someone who spends too much time at the beach.

He finishes his cigarette and reaches into his pocket for the pouch again. It seems that he intends to wait me out. I watch the glow of his cigarette, a metaphor for his breath.

He is breathing and therefore he is real.

I creep back down the corridor and there is my sister sleeping. The dark lump in the bed where she has pulled the covers up over her head. Nothing of her to be seen outside the blankets and yet her presence permeates the room even in her sleep. I pick silently through the clothing on the floor on my side of the room.

Jeans. A T-shirt. It is harder to find my bra and a pair of knickers but eventually I have it all tucked under my arm. I pull the door closed behind me, holding the handle and slowly letting it go so that there is not even a click of it closing.

I dress quickly, roll the light nightdress into a ball and hide it under the lounge. He is still here, in the soft moonlight. There is still a hot glow pointing to his mouth. I pause at the door, slide the bolt open. Closed, open. Even if he has a key he would only be able to enter the house if our grandmother forgot to slip the bolt closed, and that is impossible. The back door with its chain, the front door and its bolt. The sliding glass doors that must be locked or unlocked and then another little chain slipped across for extra protection. The house is a fortress. When I am outside the bolt will be left open. Our grandmother will know that I have gone. There is no way to cover my tracks. My heart sets up its deafening hammer-thump in my chest. My fingers shake a little as I lock the door from the outside. Locked but not bolted.

Raphael bends and rubs the glowing end of his cigarette in the dirt. He holds his hand out to show me three cigarette stubs.

'Lesson number one,' he says with a disarming wink, 'leave no trace.'

He reaches into his back pocket and when he removes his hand there is nothing but a few stray flakes of tobacco.

'The door,' I tell him. 'You can't bolt it from the outside.'

'We will be back before anyone notices.'

Raphael wipes his palm on his thigh and holds his hand out to me a second time. I put my fingers against him and like this, suddenly, he slips his fingers between mine, a thatch of skin, and we are holding hands. This is the first time I have held hands with

120

a boy. With anyone except my sister, our mother, or Oma. His fingers between mine, a delicate lacing, a gesture so intimate that I know I must be blushing, a red beacon flaring up in the dark. If he notices he doesn't mention it. He turns and drags me behind him like a boat. The air is a warm bath. Child's play, no harm. My boots snag on a clump of grass and I find I am giggling. He turns and grins and it is okay.

'Where are you taking me?'

'Don't you want to see where Emily goes?'

'I suppose.'

And I follow. It is a simple enough thing. My hand in his hand. Our fingers interlaced. The sound of his shoes and mine at a canter. The hoof-thud against dry ground. When we come to the fence between our place and the neighbour Raphael lifts his foot onto the barbed wire to clamber through. I notice that he is wearing sandshoes, thin, a little worn where the cloth meets the white rubber toe. Emily has similar shoes, and somehow this normalises him a little. He pushes down with his foot and pulls at the top rail with his fist.

'Watch the barbs.' I step gingerly through. My shirt catches and he shushes me, tells me to stop, plucks my T-shirt away from the wire.

'You're not so used to climbing through barbed-wire fences.'

'No,' I say. 'I am not used to climbing through fences at all.'

Outside there are acres and acres of other people's land. This is what I notice first, how big it all is. This is the paddock where Flame gallops and it is only now that I realise why he feels the need to throw his head back, to lift his powerful legs with such abandon. There is space here to run. Our own garden is tiny in comparison. This giant expanse of grass, with hills and a little creek and a copse of trees, is all the world. The countryside feels smaller when seen from the back seat of a moving van with your grandmother and mother in the front. Now the sky stretches from one horizon to the next and the railway track underlines the distances that must be travelled to get from one place to the next. There is a moon, full and almost orange. I notice the way things are outlined, tree branches holding light in the cups of their leaves, leaving a deep black underline below a shimmer. Of course I will wake and realise that I have been dreaming. I stoop and touch the grass. The slasher went over it only weeks ago but it is thick and ankle deep now. The grass drips moon and is wet to touch, but it has not been raining.

'What time is it now?'

He laughs. His face is creased with laughter, crumpled and folded in on itself. I don't think it was that funny just to ask the time, but I grin because watching him laugh is quite lovely.

He turns and whistles twice. The sound is piercing. Twice more, the shrill clear note and then I hear it and I know. Flame always answers to a whistle. I know this because we often call him over when we go to visit at some unexpected time. Emily can whistle more clearly than I can and she calls just as he is calling now, and Flame answers, just as he is answering now, with a staccato clapping of his feet against the ground. In the darkness the sound of his gallop is too loud. I turn back towards our side of the fence half expecting a light to flick on, my grandmother waking; or would it be worse to face Emily who might never speak to me again if she found me here?

Flame stands and stamps and nods his head. He knows me. He

snuffles at the pockets of my jeans, hoping to find treats. He seems to know Raphael too and nuzzles his hand, sniffing at his pockets until Raphael reaches in and brings out the stub end of a carrot.

'Bec.'

It is odd to hear my name spoken by this boy.

'I want you to trust me, okay?'

I nod although I don't really trust anything at all, but before I can think about it he has knotted his hand in Flame's mane and thrown his arm over the tall shoulder of the horse and hoisted himself up until he is lying flat across the horse's back. It is a simple thing for him to change his slight weight and push himself into a sitting position, bareback on the horse. He is panting and grinning and he leans towards me and stretches out his hand. I remember the neighbour's kid we met all those years ago. We have never seen him since, but sometimes Flame does not answer the call and then I know the boy is home from school, out for a ride somewhere.

I shake my head. I feel myself running into a barrier that I will not be able to cross.

'I don't know how to ride a horse,' I tell him and it sounds like a thin excuse.

'You won't be riding will you? You will be sitting up behind me like a princess.'

Sometimes when Emily wants to be mean to me she calls me Princess, but there is no malice here. Raphael stretches his hand back to take in the rump of the horse as if it were a throne and I am stepping towards it before I have time to change my mind. I am taking his hand and he is pulling me. It seems a long way up even though I suspect Flame is quite short as horses go. Raphael lifts me and I reach over Flame's back but I am slipping and I land back on my feet, off-balance, stumbling backwards, almost falling but righting myself at the last moment. Flame takes a few skittish steps and Raphael pats his neck and whispers into his mane until he settles. The boy looks so confident up there and I am suddenly certain I can make it.

'Count to three,' I say. He clasps my arm high up near the elbow and I clasp hold of his. He counts, and I leap on cue, reaching around the back of the gelding and transferring my weight until I am lying across his back. It is awkward to move from here to sitting and I have to clutch at Raphael to drag myself into the right position.

When I am finally sitting behind him, Flame takes a step back and I wobble a little as I settle. I clutch Raphael around the waist tightly; his skin is warm through the cotton. When he leans forward, nudging the horse gently with his heels to set him to a canter, I relax a little but I will not let go of his waist. He has a slim waist, like a girl's. Emily must have travelled on Flame's back. Emily must have felt the warm fur and the sharp backbone beneath, rudely separating her own legs, the slow rhythm of the boy's hips rising and falling under her fingers, the jolt of hooves thundering over uneven ground.

We ride till we come to an access road, neatly graded unlike our own. An open gate. We slow to a walk. It seems Raphael has planned this ride, opened the gate ahead of time, or else the neighbour leaves his paddock unsecured, which seems unlikely. There is a house, set back from the street but still visible. This is our closest neighbour. We pass this house in the car sometimes on the way to the post office. There are dogs here, little snarly cattle dogs that race to the fence and bark at us when we pass; it is odd to see the yard empty. The dogs are sleeping it seems, less disturbed by a walking horse than a crawling van, or else we are ghosts and their sharp noses and finely tuned ears can't detect us.

We reach the highway and the bitumen sucks up the moonlight. Raphael pulls at the horse's mane, stopping for the sleepless traffic and there is a moment when I feel unbalanced. I cling to him more tightly. Cars hush past. We wait as a road train claims all the space the highway has, one truck followed by another truck, and the lights are so loud that I duck my head down behind the safe barrier of his body. I feel the rush of air, buffeting me. Flame shifts his weight. The trucks rattle away in a fumy shout of wind and the following station wagon seems like no threat at all.

There are no lights on a horse, a problem that Raphael doesn't seem to worry about. He waits for the station wagon to pass then taps the horse into a canter. Perhaps he knows I am terrified. He holds Flame short of a gallop, which might make me vomit with fear. We keep to the side of the highway, on the gravel shoulder, but the cars still pass too close and my arms ache from keeping them so tense for so long.

On horseback it seems a long way to town. Eventually I see the light from the motel sign flashing, one bulb at a time flicking on, then three long dashes of light like neon Morse code before the whole pattern starts all over again. Raphael turns the horse's head up the hill by the shut-up shop. This is a part of the town I have never seen before. The low wooden houses, the picket fences, the feed sheds and stringy rose bushes struggling against the climate.

'Where are we going?' I find that I am shouting unnecessarily. We clop up the side street in a lull in the traffic and the world has returned to its midnight silence.

'A surprise.'

Raphael kicks Flame gently in the ribs and we are galloping for the first time and Raphael is tipping his head back and aiming a joyful shout at the sky above.

'Come on,' he yells back at me, 'do this!'

And the sound that comes out of his throat is a dingo's howl, deep and canine and aimed at the blowsy moon.

I hold my head up and feel the rush of warm air through my hair and the steady thump, thump, thump of my bottom bouncing up and down against the bare back of the horse and I open my mouth, intending to howl with him, but this is not a dream. This is real. Raphael is not a figment of whatever madness is troubling my sister. And I close my lips and duck down behind his shoulders again without making a sound.

I wonder if it is illegal to ride a horse on the road after dark. I wonder if, like with a bicycle, you are supposed to wear some kind of a helmet. I listen for approaching sirens. I am not the rule breaker in our family. If it weren't that my sister had been here before me I wouldn't be doing this at all.

He pulls off the highway suddenly. I wonder if you are supposed to indicate when you are riding a horse. It is possible that we are breaking multiple traffic laws, a domino effect, a tumbling of wrongdoings, starting with his appearance in our bedroom and ending here, in the crazy race down a grassed hill. And now I do scream as he wanted me to scream, my mouth as full as the moon and all the bright glare of my terror shining out in a howl, more cat than canine. So I yowl and cling to his waist and he runs the horse in a sharp little circle to a sudden halt almost, but not quite, unbalancing us next to a wall with a mural painted on it.

'Hup,' he says, meaning down. I freeze. 'Hold on to me tightly and swing your left leg over. I won't fall off.' But he very nearly does, taking the whole weight of me and crouching down over the neck of the animal for balance. He slips gracefully down after me and my thighs are numb from the pounding. I rub at them, trying to get some feeling back.

Raphael stretches his hands out to take in the wall, the grass, the buildings beyond. The school. There is a playground in one corner, sprint lanes etched out in white paint on the grass. There are banks of stairs covered by a corrugated roof where children must sit when there is a sports day or maybe an outdoor performance. Behind these the buildings are low and uniform and linked by paths each covered by the same corrugated metal.

'Is this your school?' I ask, although I am sure the school only goes to grade ten, and I am certain now that he is the same age as my sister, maybe reaching the end of grade twelve.

Raphael shrugs. 'Tonight,' he tells me, 'this is our school.'

When he takes my hand his touch is an electric shock. We run together across the grassed area and climb the stairs and when we are perched on top my heart is racing. I am unused to so much space, so much running. No one can see me except my sister's secret friend.

When I have caught my breath he is leaning back, his arms stretched out, clutching the still-warm concrete.

'Is this where you bring my sister?'

He nods.

127

'And what? Do you break in to the classrooms? Write your names on the walls? Steal money from the teacher's desk?'

'No,' he says, and when I ask him what they do here, my sister and the boy that I thought might be her imaginary friend, he leans close and puts a hand on the back of my head and kisses me. It goes on until my mouth is his mouth, my tongue is his tongue, our breaths intertwined as our hands are knotted together.

When there is no breath left in us, all air spent, he pulls away and smiles and pushes a lock of my hair away from my face. I think for a moment he might say something. I cannot; the kiss has taken all the breath out of me. But he doesn't speak at all. Instead he leans forward and his mouth is against mine, gently this time, nipping at the edges of my lips, and I learn the truth of it. That he is definitely not imaginary at all.

Make Believe Kisses

We paint John from memory. I have no photographs of him, which serves to underline the illicit nature of the affair. I can barely believe we ever made love. When we paint his left hand I remember the fingers slipping inside me, the frantic rhythm as he pushed them in and out. Fingering. A childish word, a thing that teenagers do in the school yard, the thing that Raphael did to me beside the deserted assembly hall. The smell of horse on his skin, the glow of a full moon helping to show us what was happening.

We paint John's hand so that two of his fingers, the middle two, the fingering ones, are pushed together. He whispered to me, never breaking his rhythm. He told me I was really wet and his words summoned another spill of juices from inside me. I closed my eyes but opened them almost immediately as I felt his tongue reach out to taste.

This moment is here in our painting, the press of his painted fingers, my imminent orgasm captured in his smug smile. *I know I can bring a girl to orgasm,* he said, and I remember this as we swap to the finest brush and touch the canvas lightly to underline the creasing of skin beside his smiling eyes. We paint his right hand only it is not a hand. I thought I would paint him as a bear but I suppose she sees him differently. The hoof is as we remember it, dark with a series of cracks near the base of it. The hair is neat and brown and peeks out from under his sleeve. We remember lying near a horse's hooves and watching the little cracks in them. We remember flinching as a horse stomped at the bare ground. We remember Raphael fingering me and how I flinched then, too, because it hurt. The harder he pushed, the faster the rhythm, the more I flinched and the startled wonder on his face as he held his hand up to the moonlight looking at the colour there. We paint the blood on his fingers, then. The same colour as the tips of the flames eating at the hem of his jeans and at his hooves.

When we are finished she signs the painting with her name, Emily Reich. A perfect match to the signature she makes without me. I step back and look at the painting from a little distance. If only I could paint this way, the skill in the detail, the quality of light. There is a reason my sister has become an icon of modern Australian art. I look at my fingers, flecked with blue and smelling of turpentine. This canvas will be dry before I leave and I will put it in the alcove with the other Emily Reichs. I will hide the alcove behind a stack of my own, inferior works, a treasure trove of paintings that no one will ever see but me: the Emily Reichs I have painted over the years, the Emily Reichs that my psychiatrist warned me not to paint.

I lock all the windows and all the doors. For a time, when I left home, I could not sleep unless the locks were in place. I thought I might see Raphael standing in the middle of the room, unannounced and uninvited. Even vampires must receive an invitation; hallucinations, it seems, are not quite so polite. If he suddenly appeared I would have been frightened, but to be truthful I would have been a little excited too.

I lock all the windows and all the doors and I sit up on the couch, staring, hoping. I am hoping for John, I suppose, but it is easy to make the leap to that other visitor. They have something in common of course. John is a wonderful kisser. There have been other boys, not boys, men. Since I left home I have slept with older men, men with beards with flecks of grey, and deep forceful voices. Men who have erectile problems or prostate problems or backs that are shot. Older men who are nothing like anything from my childhood.

Once a woman sat next to me at a bar and bought me a drink and flirted. I left before the drink arrived. That acrid sweaty scent in the cab, only realising that it was the scent of my own panic when I stepped out into my driveway. I called the psych in the middle of the night but it went to message bank even though she had said I could call her any time. I locked the windows and bolted them, I remember this. I drank vodka till I vomited and then I was morose till dawn, sleeping all weekend and still hung-over on the Monday, or maybe just exhausted from throwing up so much.

Tonight I will not repeat that mistake. I look at the bottle of wine in the refrigerator and leave it where it is. No, it has not escaped my notice that John is a young man, a boy, not a teenager, as Raphael was a teenager, but I have learned to think and double-think my actions. There is no psych now to call at odd hours. I am done with all that, I am cured. Still I haul my knees up into the hug of my arms and I wait, pretending it is John I am waiting for.

I wonder what time it is in Beijing.

PART TWO

Arriving in Beijing

In the plane, after what seems like a week, we are finally making our descent. A young woman has fallen asleep, leaning forward in her seat. She has been snorting through blocked sinuses. A cold she has been harbouring for the whole flight has finally set in. I have watched it slowly overtake her, a sniffle at first, a dabbing at her nose with a tissue. She has been lethargic throughout the trip, falling in and out of sleep with annoying tinny music chiming from her earbuds for most of the way from Singapore.

A sneeze drags her out of dream and launches her into the waking world. She fumbles in her pocket for another tissue, wipes her face, massages under her eyes to ease her sinuses, presses the flat expanse of her cheeks. Something to do with the change in pressure has caused her pain. More pain as we lose altitude. She presses her face, her eyes widen in distress, she pushes at her jaw. I have been trying not to catch her eye but now she reaches for my arm, pushing one hand to her mouth, massaging her jaw.

'All my teeth ache,' she says to me. Her accent is German. I am reminded suddenly of my grandmother.

'Don't worry, we'll be there soon,' I whisper, but it is little comfort. I watch as she writhes in her seat and just before touchdown she stares at me, her eyes imploring, her hands pressed to her face and I am reminded of that painting by Munch. There is nothing I can do to help. I sit with my seatbelt low and tight and watch.

I take this relentless unease with me when I stand and slip my backpack on my shoulders and sidestep out into the aisle, leaving the woman to dab at her smudged eye shadow and blow her nose into the darkly smeared tissue, finally released from the terror of her descent.

Emily isn't waiting for me. I search the crowd of faces and there are a handful of westerners but their presence is eclipsed by the multitudes of Chinese people calling out to loved ones, wrangling stray children. They press against the barrier and shout. It seems like the cries are in anger, but despite the volume and tone of their greetings, they grin or laugh or at the very most seem mildly irritated.

There is a sign for the taxi. I heft my suitcase and begin the long descent. I have barely slept and my back feels like it has been crushed into a small box for the long hours of flights and transits. I rest my bag on the bottom of the first flight of stairs, stretch my fingers out carefully. A patch of sweat is gathering where my backpack touches my skin. I should have brought something to tie up my hair. The curls are already turning into a nest of dark leeches, sucking the moisture from my neck.

At the bottom of three more flights there is a taxi rank that seems to stretch out forever. Dozens of yellow cabs side by side and men in uniforms with flags ushering the slow blinking travellers into a stockyard of metal barriers. I follow the waving flags the length of two city blocks. I wait. Surely the man with the flag will move me to the appropriate taxi. There are other passengers jumping past me, ignoring the possibility of a queue. I step off the sidewalk onto the bitumen, heft my bag. I head towards a cab and the man with the uniform and flag steps up to wave me away. He says something to me in Mandarin and when I stare at him blankly he points abruptly to a cab further down the line. I aim myself at it, dragging my bag behind me. I stash the suitcase in the boot and climb into the front beside the driver.

'Nee how.' My only words. Then I hold the map up and point to the place where my sister lives. The driver pushes the map away, says something in Mandarin, sighs.

'Shajing Hutong.' There is an email in my phone. I retrieve it, point to the Chinese characters. 'Shajing Hutong.'

He shrugs, which may or may not mean 'yes' and then we are moving finally out of the airport and onto the road.

I reach for the seatbelt but there is none. The driver has a belt hanging beside him but makes no move to buckle himself in. He sees me searching and laughs, makes a waving motion with his hand. I clutch at the leather handhold, adjusting to the idea of speed without protection.

The cab is airconditioned but I can feel the heat of the day seeping in from outside the window. The driver presses something on the dash and there is a message recorded in Mandarin followed by the words, 'Thank you for enjoying Beijing cab. We are happy to help you to find your location.'

I check my map. The maze of streets spreads out to the edges of the page. I have no idea where the airport is in relation to the red dot I have marked. I lean my head back onto the hard seat and close my eyes.

The cab jolts to a stop. I sit up, startled. The driver laughs and points to the numbers. Two hundred on the meter. I reach behind to where I have stashed my backpack, find my wallet and the unfamiliar notes. Mao's face stares officiously out from each one.

I struggle out of the cab and open my map. We must be there, wherever there is. A street sign in Mandarin but beneath the Chinese characters are letters that I recognise. I check the word against the map and find the corresponding street. A small victory. My sister's place is here, somewhere behind the row of shops. I shoulder my backpack and drag my bag behind me. The footpath is cracked and patched but there is an entryway and the sign says Shajing Hutong. I drag my things up onto the cobbled surface.

The road is lined by trees that arc over to touch fingers; the cracked shingles of a roof are tipped with gorgeous grey tiles. Manhole covers are pressed with delicate patterns of circles and lines. The bicycles ring their bells constantly, everything in slow but constant motion, everything rattling or ringing or shouting. A motorcycle honks and I step to the side to let it pass. There are people here, but not as many as on the main street. Doors are red and faded green and purple, chipped and rusted. The place smells. Not a pleasant tree-lined odour, but harsh scents of petrol and piss.

I stare at the map, turn into a cross-street. The alley seems to become narrower. At the end of it are large red doors, slightly ajar, with knockers shaped like dragon heads. A dog barks from inside an adjacent doorway. I push one of the doors and there is an entryway behind. A potplant sags before two glass doors with elaborate metal frameworks. No curtains, no privacy. I heft my bag up and over the entry step. Emily's door is the one on the right. I realise that I am holding my breath. I breathe out before I knock.

Then there is Emily.

She reaches towards me and gives me a kind of hug, at an angle, a little side-press and a tap of her hand on my back before she pulls away. The same clear sharp eyes, but the shape of them is outlined by dark circles. She is heavier, with something overblown about her skin as if she has been suddenly inflated. She looks taut and mottled. Her top has shoestring straps and the skin on her upper arms is dimpled and picked at, scabbed over in places.

I am shocked to see her this way, blown out and hidden under her own flesh, and this meeting is so many things: a death, a revelation, a gift that shrugs off its festive wrapping only to disappoint. This moment is also a mirror and I am reflected: I am this size, this weight. I am this same embodiment of jetlagged exhaustion. In her eyes I find my own loneliness and insecurities.

I recover quickly, hiding behind the polite smile that I wear to classes, and she smiles back, one half of her mouth still drawn down into a frown of consternation. If you held your hand up to obscure half her face you would see politeness on one side and nothing but sorrow when you moved your hand over to the other.

The heat is startling. Even the hottest Brisbane days have not prepared me for it. I have stripped off my jumper but my dress feels like a blanket. The little half-sleeves cling damply to my upper arms. The fabric hangs heavily across my chest. My bra itches.

'Hey,' she says.

And I say, 'Hey.'

'Good to see you.'

'Same.'

Her voice is the only thing I recognise completely. There were photos of her, of course. It was impossible not to see these pictures staring out at me from the racks in art bookshops, once even leaping out from the television. When I did see them they held me transfixed. I stared at the pale beautiful woman, the girl grown tall and more glamorous. This was at the beginning of her notoriety, and once I had started to look at her I could not stop. I gathered up every magazine. I started to leave the television on in the background, stopping to check so regularly that even I could sense a growing obsession. I could have tracked her through the gossip columns, photograph by photograph. Instead I bundled the magazines I had collected into the recycling bin. Every so often I would come across a treatise on Emily's work in the *Art Monthly*, a retrospective in one of the journals I subscribe to. I would be confronted by new work, each painting darker and richer than the next.

But in general I have not seen a photograph of my sister since that brief period when I saw the edges of myself blurring, waking at odd hours in the night, expecting to see my sister grown older and more exquisite leaning over my bed. This Emily, here and now, is a different creature entirely.

She stretches her hand out almost apologetically to take in the small immaculate room. White walls, white leather lounge chairs. A handful of paintings lean against one of the walls, neatly stacked one in front of another. There is a line of shoes beside the door and I wonder suddenly if I should have taken my own shoes off. The floor is tiled but perhaps I am tracking dust into her house.

'White is the colour of death,' she says, 'at least it is in China. I hung white lanterns in the courtyard when I first arrived but my neighbour made me take them down. I'm not responsible for the walls or the colour of the lounge chairs. Someone else made that mistake for me.'

She reaches out to take the satchel off my shoulder and there is an awkward moment when I abandon the weight of it and it almost falls from her hands. She moves the bag into one corner and I wheel my suitcase in beside it.

She stands for a moment and I see her eyes travel down my body, but it is impossible to tell which side of her face best expresses her judgment. When she has taken in the length and breadth of me she opens her mouth as if there is something she is about to say. This is the moment where politeness demands a compliment, but she exhales and is otherwise silent.

'You look good,' I say and both of us know this is a lie. My sister's silence was more honest. I notice a narrowing of her eyes and feel chastised.

'Coffee?' she asks. 'Or do you want a shower straight up. The flight…'

'Both sound good.'

'Both, then.'

She points to a narrow alcove at the side of a tiny kitchenette. The shower is no bigger than a camp shower, a small corner unit with curved glass doors. I notice that one of the panes is missing and there is a crust of crumbly glass clinging to the metal frame.

I feel like a giant in her bathroom. When I turn sideways my hips bridge the distance between the sink and the wall. I stare into the mirror, to see if the stray dark hairs have begun to grow back on my chin, but the closer I get the more indistinct the image. There is something wrong with the mirror, some design fault. I step back, shed my clothing. I am glad that the image is not too sharp. There is a ledge above the sink and her body products are lined up neatly there. Brands I recognise but have never used.

When I step into the shower I am mammoth. There is barely any room to turn. The water ricochets off my skin and out of the broken panel. I stand under the shower and allow myself to indulge in a short burst of tears.

I emerge from the shower presentable. I brush my teeth and rinse the toothbrush under the running water. I put on lipstick.

My sister is tucked up in one of the big white couches. She nods to a cup of coffee that she has left steaming on the table.

'White and one?'

I haven't used sugar for years but I nod anyway. The coffee smells good and strong. The comfort of the familiar. I sip.

'I've missed you,' she says then, staring into her coffee. It would be a complicated lie to tell her that I have missed her too and so I move over towards her paintings.

'May I?'

She nods. I lift and turn the first canvas. It is taller than I am and heavy. I lean it against the wall. It is our grandmother. It is such a shock to see her this way. Her face is perfectly symmetrical, without any slackness or drooping. Our grandmother before the stroke. Our Oma. Her mouth has that same tightness of lip that I remember, her gaze sharp as diamond. She is sitting on a throne and dressed in Chinese robes, yellow silk. It is not a colour that flatters her; the softness of the fabric somehow underlines the harshness of her expression. The robes drop down over her lap and the hem hangs just above where her ankles are, bony furred ankles, hard cracked hooves beneath. This little detail changes the image from something that might be a tribute to something born out of the darkest corners of mythology. The hoof of a demon, the hoof of a sprite in human form.

'For the exhibition?'

She shrugs. 'No. They're for you. Happy birthday.'

It is overwhelming. I glance at the stack of canvases, five of them, four still burying their faces against the blank wall.

'I can't take these.'

'I've already booked the courier and paid for it.'

'Emily, it's not about the money, it's just…' John's voice in my head, *Do you know how much these are worth?* 'Don't they have to go to a museum or something?'

Emily snorts, 'It's not like they're heritage listed.'

I reach out to turn the second canvas but she struggles out of the soft white lounge chair and grabs my arm.

'Come on, you'll just embarrass me if you look at them now. Wanna go see some China?'

'Sure.'

'Not too tired?'

'No,' I say, although my limbs ache and if I closed my eyes now I would be asleep in seconds. 'Not too tired yet.'

She squeezes my arm so hard that I flinch. 'It's good to see you, Bec. I really have missed you.'

'I've missed you too,' I say.

I gulp the last of the coffee, which burns the roof of my mouth a little. When I put my empty cup down on the side table she hands me a heavy D lock and a key.

'Right-o,' Emily says. 'Let's get on our bikes.'

Riding a bicycle in Beijing is taking a leap of faith. There are road rules, it seems: most of the cars stick to one side of the road. When there is a red light some of the cars stop. There is an area at the side of the street that seems to be reserved for bicycles and mopeds except sometimes a car pushes down the narrow space and then the motorcycles and bicycles crawl to a stop, people step off their vehicles and drag them up onto the footpath which also seems to be a place for bicycles and mopeds and the occasional car.

It has been years since I rode a bike and this one is too low even for my short legs. The chain is rusted. When I put the brakes on, which is something I do every ten feet or so, there is a loud screech. When I reach for the bell, which is also a constant necessity, I have to let go of the handlebars briefly and the bike wobbles. At an intersection I step off and wait for my sister to lead the way. It seems the push of traffic is endless.

'Sometimes,' she says, 'I close my eyes and just ride out into the traffic. It's the only way to get across. There's one unshakable rule in Beijing—don't hit anyone. You have to trust that the cars are trying not to kill you. Okay, *now*,' she says, and it seems that several bicycles have chosen this moment to make a break for it. I follow, weaving slightly, keeping an eye on my sister's back. If I lose her I will never find my way to her house. I am overwhelmed by the size of this place, the sheer volume of cars all sliding to a halt to avoid the bicycles.

Emily stops suddenly, resting one foot on the sidewalk. The

English words Aroma Fashion are printed on the window under a string of Chinese characters. She locks her bike and I lift mine up onto the footpath beside it.

'This girl's okay,' she steps up over the entryway. 'She designs and makes the stuff. Mostly ripped off from pictures in magazines. But at least she picks good magazines.'

It is quieter inside this shop. The woman sitting behind the counter is wearing red chiffon. Her hair is pulled back into a severe bun. She is the first carefully dressed Chinese woman I have seen. I realise now, as I look at her neatly tailored silk shirt, that the streets are packed with people who seem to have dressed in their oldest functional clothes. Ugly cotton prints, loose shorts, old patched sandals. Something about her neatness is jarring. There are patches of dark sweat in my armpits, a vague damp smell from under my hair. I can feel a fine layer of dirt gathering on my skin.

'*Ni hao*,' my sister greets the shop assistant, says something else in Mandarin. A smile and a response. My sister has managed to learn some of the language, enough to have a quick conversation. I remember the lessons she used to run at the side of the house when our grandmother was not watching and feel the wave of memory reach up and lift me away, the unfamiliar sound of Mandarin replaced suddenly by the odd clipped Elvish syllables.

In bed some nights Emily would read to me. We had finished *The Hobbit* and we had moved on to *The Lord of the Rings*. There was a wonderful secret pleasure in knowing a language that only existed in books: a language shared between the two of us and barely anyone else in the world. Elves were her favourite. They are quiet and lithe and beautiful and they ride their white horses bareback, which is how she wanted to ride if she could have ridden at all. Our grandmother knew three languages. I once reminded Emily of this and her mouth hardened to a pencil line of condescension. Even if our grandmother knew twenty languages she would not be invited to share in our Elvish. This was something for my sister and me alone.

The shop assistant quickly presses a button and I hear the low whir of an airconditioning unit cranking up.

'They only put the aircon on for westerners,' Emily tells me as if this is a fact that needs no explanation. I wonder at her ease with this odd racial inequality.

She picks up a hanger, a high-waisted green dress with cute little straps. 'Try this on.'

I feel my chest tighten.

'What size is it?'

'It says large. It'll fit. It's way too big on me. I think it will fit you nicely. Try it on.'

I look at the round swell of her hips, the thick set of her shoulders. Surely she must be the same size as I am now. Maybe I am deluded. Maybe I am even bigger than I think. I feel myself swell to the size of the most obese person I can imagine. I could be the size of a baby elephant, I could be a whale. My sister certainly thinks I am the size of a whale.

'I don't need clothes. I have clothes.'

'I want to get you something. For the opening.'

'No. You've given me too much already. I didn't bring you anything.'

'Yeah, but I've got all this money. People pay me stupid prices for my paintings now. Do you know how much they sell for? It's ridiculous. I know how much they pay you at university.'

'Emily,' I snap, more forcefully than I intended, 'I'm not going to try clothes on.'

There is a flash of the old Emily, the dark brooding stare, the potential for damage. I find myself shrinking away from her. I remember a time when she picked up her cupboard and threw it over to my side of the room, the terrible crack as something broke, what was that? A plastic container filled with oil pastels, I think; the sound has stayed with me anyway.

Then there is that half smile. Emily holds the emerald dress up to the light.

'It's nice. I think it's a Collette Dinnigan. Or a reinterpretation of one. I saw it in *Australian Vogue*. I think. Or maybe it was *Who Weekly*. How's that? *Vogue* or *Who Weekly*. Interchangeable. Talk about a global village.'

'Emily.'

She smiles vaguely at me.

I tell her, 'I'm sorry, I just don't want to try dresses on right now.'

'Have you got something to wear to the opening?'

'Yes.'

'Not a red dress I hope, I am going to wear red, or maybe it would be good to dress the same, matching red dresses to prove that we are sisters. What colour is your dress?'

'Black.'

'Maybe I should get a black dress to match.'

'I'm tired,' I tell her.

'Collette Dinnigan.' She checks the tag. 'For two hundred kuai. Do you know what that works out to? Thirty bucks—something like that. Collette would vomit, don't you think?'

Emily puts the dress back on the rack wistfully. 'Chinese girls are little sticks,' she says suddenly. 'No tits.' I glance at the stylish shop assistant who seems unfazed by my sister's rudeness. 'You got tits so early. I was always jealous about that.'

'Really?'

'You've let your hair grow.' She reaches out with one finger as if she is about to touch a stray lock of my hair. I am not sure which one of us flinches first but her hand is snatched back before making contact.

'I liked the asymmetrical thing better. I think.'

And it seems impossible that she would know about the asymmetrical haircut I endured for a handful of months.

'But I suppose you need the length to balance a fatter face.'

My sister says something to the shopkeeper and walks out to our bikes. I gaze up into a sky that is a haze of grey. Something drips onto my cheek and I brush it away.

'Is it going to rain?'

'Doubt it. Oh, they spray the trees with something. You are always getting dripped on. Toxic chemicals probably, no worse than the pollution I suppose. Acid rain. You'll notice there's no bugs. Nothing alive at all. I try not to think about that too much. We're breathing this shit in, I've been doing it for over a year. You know how hard it is to kill a cockroach?'

She looks back over her shoulder at me. I shudder under her gaze. She looks up and then down, flattening me into my component parts. I smooth down my skirt over my huge thighs. I wish she had dragged me away to a colder country. There would be sleeves and coats and thick wool tights to hide behind.

'We might have to take you to a tailor. Get something made.'

'It's okay. I have clothes.'

'I want to get you something. Let me get you something.'

'You got me a ticket to China.'

'China. Can you believe that? China. My little sister is here. With me. In China.'

She laughs and steps up on to the pedals and rings her bell as she launches herself out into the nightmare of oncoming bicycles. She is larger now, but still just as graceful. I follow at a halting pace, dodging, stopping, pulling over onto the footpath. It is easy enough to keep track of my sister. She is a gorgeous flash of blue shining against the drab background of shapeless cotton frocks and dirty T-shirts. She is other-worldly and exciting and for a moment I am overwhelmed with pride.

Beijing Art

We dodge old ladies and running children, we swerve past buses and taxi cabs. We are overtaken by an old man with a huge pile of rice bags on the back of his bicycle. Sometimes she waits for red lights, sometimes she darts through without pause. I hold my breath and follow her even when it means I am almost run over by a moped. I shout apologies and I am not sure if they are heard or understood because I am pedalling fast, trying to keep up. She pulls up outside a building in a long line of buildings. Swings her leg off the bike and leans it against a tree. She locks the wheel to the frame.

'No one's going to steal them anyway, but you can lock your bike to mine. I do that. It makes me feel a little safer.' She sweeps her hair away from her face. 'We have to do this lunch thing. I would skip it if I could but…' she shrugs. I struggle with the D lock. The key is rusty and I wiggle it uselessly before it finally clicks open.

When I turn to find her she has disappeared. I stand on the

footpath and there are dozens of people teeming past. When I look out to the street there are all the cars and bikes and scooters. So many people. I feel my heart racing. I have never seen so many people in the one place. It is impossible to tell how many lanes of traffic are racing by, just a mass of vehicles and shoulder-to-shoulder pedestrians. A few shops away a small child is playing in a puddle of water, crouched down, and concentrating intensely on whatever she is picking out of the water. Glass. I shudder. There is a woman sitting on a stool near her, I assume this is her mother, and yet she makes no move to stop the child from picking up the fragments of glass, piling them up on a scrap of paper.

The light is gently fading. I am hungry, but I can't remember if it is late at night back home or early afternoon. I have a terrible sense of displacement. What would John be doing at this time? Is he in class? I have lost track of the days.

The restaurant is packed and it takes me a minute to find her. A waiter shouts something at me. I wish I had learned the Mandarin for 'I don't understand'. I shake my head, hoping that the gesture and my expression will be universal. I see a flash of colour and it is her. She is sitting at a table with a group of westerners. One Chinese girl among them wearing an eighties style cropped denim jacket and high-waisted denim shorts. They are all flamboyantly dressed, most of them in structured black skirts or cute little fifties frocks. All of them slim, pretty girls in their thirties. I am reminded of my students, so carefully dressed with their outrageous haircuts. I am glad now that I let mine grow out, at least I will not look like I am trying to be one of them.

I stand awkwardly beside my sister's chair. There is no chair for me to sit on and for a moment I imagine that I was meant to wait outside with the bikes. The Chinese girl stands and grabs one from another table.

'Park your arse, Bec,' she says in such a broad Australian accent that I suppose I look startled. The Chinese girl laughs. 'Yeah, and I don't speak any Mandarin either. You should see some of the locals, shouting and shouting, then I say "G'day mate" and they look at me like I'm an alien.'

I sit on the chair she offers me. She knows my name but I don't know hers.

'How's the flight?'

Another girl, a pale blonde curly-haired angel. She is smoking a cigarette and ashes it onto the floor. There are people smoking at some of the other tables too. I can hear the sound of crickets chirping. I turn to see where it is coming from but there are just other tables, locals shouting at each other as if they're angry. One old woman leans away from her chair and spits onto the floor. I feel light headed.

'Okay. Long. I got some reading done.'

'You're a teacher right? Teach art?'

They know all about me and I don't even know their names.

My sister looks past them. I remember that look, that distant preoccupation like she is watching television, captivated by something happening outside the parameters of the world. I shift nervously in my chair.

'Yes. At university.'

'The next wave,' says a little nuggety, spike-haired girl in a mean singlet top. 'Discovered any geniuses yet? Genii? Anyone we should look out for?'

I think about John. I could tell them about John, drop his

name, pave the way for him, but I know that I will betray my feelings if I even mention him so I shake my head.

'Couple of good artists in the making. Some good work. Lots of not-so-good work. You know how it is.'

They laugh. The smoking girl lights another cigarette off the first.

'Hey, congrats on your exhibition. Awesome review, Nancy would have been green with jealousy. I went to uni with Nancy.' She rolls her eyes.

I am so startled that I can't think of anything to say. Ed told me to get the papers. I wonder what they said.

'So you all got the floor plan?' She turns back towards the table in general.

The Chinese girl sighs. 'I want to order first. I'm hungry. Is anyone else hungry?'

Some nods, some shrugs. I pick up the menu in front of me and there are photographs with Chinese characters beside them. Nothing is familiar. I look towards Emily but she is still staring off into the middle distance. She is the same age now as our mother was. Same age, same overblown flesh, same vacant stare. I feel a little leap in my chest and glance down at the menu once more.

The girl with the cigarette shouts something and I flinch at her tone, so confident and perhaps a little condescending. She waves her cigarette in the air and a waiter races to her side. I listen to them ordering, everyone with words for what they are after. When it comes time for my sister to order she turns to the waiter slowly and drags herself back into the real world. This is the sister of my childhood and I remember. I can feel a growing sense of unease settling on my shoulders tightening into a knot at the base of my neck.

She speaks to the waiter quietly, calmly, she points in my direction and there are more words in Mandarin. The waiter laughs and nods at me. Emily shrugs and talks and then when she is done she smiles vaguely and says, 'I've ordered a few things you might like unless you had something particular…?'

'No,' I tell her, and, 'thanks.' She smiles at me briefly and I lean towards her. She is my anchor here.

When the orders have been placed and the menus collected, the girl with the cigarette slaps a folder down onto the table.

It is a familiar conversation, logistics, meterage, hanging requirements. She produces a spreadsheet and I glance at the paper that is put in front of Emily. Some of the names are familiar. Artists. I have seen some of their work in magazines. A who's who of the brave new voices on the Australian scene. Emily will have the whole of the lower floor.

The girl with the cigarette takes out an iPad and a keyboard and there is some discussion about the placement of Australian artists within the context of the wider Asian community. I read the major arts magazines. I understand their arguments, I can even interpret the impenetrable language, but I feel my vision clouding and I am certain that my vague half-smile is the same expression as my sister's. Just us against the world.

Our food arrives and Emily stirs. She places her hand on my thigh, a sign of camaraderie. She points to each dish and explains what is being placed on the table: jasmine flowers stir-fried in a spicy sauce, deep fried cheese from a particular province, grated potato, chicken, beef, fish.

'When you look in the rivers around here you can sometimes see the fish,' she whispers to me. 'Huge fish, gasping at the surface. You could reach out and pick them up in your hand. Sometimes I want to scoop them out just to put them out of their misery, but they are huge, the thickness of your arm or bigger. Somehow they have struggled this way through a long and difficult life. And quite a lot of industrial effluent.'

'Thanks Emily.' The woman with the cigarette drops the butt on the floor and tamps it out with her foot. She picks up the plate of fish fillets. 'Anyone for the seafood?'

They laugh, but I sense that they are wary of Emily. I lean closer to my sister to underline the fact that we are together. My sister picks up her chopsticks and picks some fish off the plate, a piece for me, a piece for her.

'Should we have ordered rice?' I ask her.

'No. Rice comes at the end if we're still hungry when all the food is gone. Rice is just to fill you up. If you're rich, like we are, then you shouldn't need the rice at all.'

I look around the room. The other diners are dressed in dowdy house frocks, crumpled old shirts, T-shirts with faded pictures on the front of them. We are like a table full of peacocks and I notice that the locals glance in our direction as if we were the floor show.

The food is good, surprisingly good. I am not a fan of Chinese food back home, which is often too glutinous or salty for me. Here the flavours are delicate and when the bill comes I make the conversion in my head and am surprised by how cheap it all is. We didn't need rice at all. I am full, and, suddenly, exhausted. I take out my wallet but Emily waves it away. She pays for the whole table. No one argues. I suppose, like John, they have all heard about Sotheby's.

'Okay chums. See you all when we saddle up.' Emily grins and I know she is taking the piss but they don't seem to realise this.

The sound of crickets becomes an almost deafening shriek and I look up to see a row of little bamboo cages hung above the doorway. I am too short to see into them but I assume the insects are trapped inside.

It is dark outside but no cooler. I struggle with the D lock. Whole families are sitting near the doors of their still-open shops, squatting on tiny stools, fanning themselves, playing card games, chatting. An old lady is bent over her embroidery. A young man digs at a machine part with a metal tool. A toddler jumps up and down in a plastic tub with some water in the bottom, clapping his hands as his shorts soak up the wet. We step onto the bikes and this is nice, this riding beside my sister.

Perhaps I am disoriented, but it seems that we have turned the wrong corner. I have a sense that we are not heading in the direction we came from. My sister rides a little way ahead of me and no matter how hard I pedal I can't seem to catch up. She turns down an even smaller lane. Doors flank the way, some of them with candles sputtering in jam jars in little alcoves. I am completely lost. She hops off the bike while it is still in motion, cruising to a stop perched on one pedal. I come to a careful halt, my brakes squealing horribly, and there is all that fuss with the bike lock to go through.

Qingdao bar is tiny and empty.

'Hey.' Emily nods to the Chinese bartender.

'Hey,' she grins back.

'Isabel, this is my sister.'

The woman leans over the bar and shakes my hand. 'Nice to meet you, sister.' A strong, firm grip. Another Australian accent from an Asian face. 'What can I get you?'

Emily steers me towards a table. 'Two Mao specials for me and my sister.' Isabel takes out the equipment, a bowl, some herbs, a mortar and pestle, a shaker and a tray of ice. She reaches for the bottles of alcohol and a plastic container of juice, lime juice perhaps, the stuff is a lurid green colour.

'You'll like this,' Emily tells me. 'Not sweet.'

I try to imagine back to our childhood. There was never a drop of alcohol in our grandmother's house. I am not sure how she knows that I don't like my cocktails sweet.

She says, 'Do you remember when you ate that whole nutmeg because I told you it was used as a drug in some countries?'

'No.'

'You grated it up, the whole thing. And then you said you were stoned.'

'I don't remember. It doesn't sound very much like me.'

'You were always doing stuff like that. Like when you did that steeplechase?'

I remember the steeplechase. I remember how she told me that horses died, riders died. She said this as she set the jumps for us to hurdle. When a horse fell and broke its legs they would shoot it dead where it was, pointing a gun right at its brain. I remember her saying this.

'No. That was you with the steeplechase.'

'Sure. I set the jumps up but you were the one who did it. I just stood at the edge and watched.'

157

That's not how it was at all. I remember it so vividly it might be yesterday. I remember her winning, and how slow and stupid I felt when I gave up jumping and just stepped over each of the makeshift jumps.

The drinks arrive in tall frosted glasses, I can smell the alcohol, gin perhaps, a hint of lemon.

'Maybe I did the nutmeg, I don't remember, but the steeple-chase was you.'

'You were pretty brave.'

'I was set upon.'

She laughs. 'I was proud when I read about your show.'

'What show?'

'You know, with the posers, Nancy what's-her-face—'

'Gato.'

'And the paedophile geek-boy.'

'I can't believe you read about that.'

'Becca, the world is the tiniest little place. In London I bumped into this boy who was in the cage next door to mine for a whole month. What are the odds of that?'

She turns slow circles around her ear and I am stumped for a moment until I realise she is making the sign for madness. The cage must be the psych unit she was kept in, a locked ward. I hold my glass more firmly. Van Gogh and his ear, Fairweather and his raft, Emily and her hot air balloon.

'So. Was it public art?'

'The dirigible?'

I nod, although the story I heard was about a hot air balloon made of all of the canvases that were in her hotel room, glued or sewn together. I shudder when I imagine the height she fell from.

'Nah,' she says. 'Transportation. But I want to hear about your exhibition. The critics raved about your work. I bet Nancy Thingo was furious. All that hype and bluster. Then someone comes and blows it all away with some great paintings. Did you enjoy yourself?'

There is a slow thudding in my temples.

'Not really.'

'Well, we'll have to fix that. This one will be loads of fun. I am so glad you came. I was hoping you would.'

She holds her glass up and bumps it against mine.

We talk about art. My art first, which is a surprise. She knows a few of my paintings and I can't imagine how she managed to see pictures of them at all.

'The internet,' she says, 'is an amazing place.'

We talk about her art. She seems less interested in this.

'No one sees my art anymore,' she says. 'They just see my signature on the bottom of the canvas.' I glance down at the table, refusing to meet her eye.

In the toilet I feel my shoulders relax a little. A vague pain behind my temple. There is a sign telling me to put my paper in the basket not in the toilet bowl. The basket is full of paper. There is a suspicious smell from inside it, urine and shit and I try not to look too closely inside it to where some of the paper is streaked with blood. The walls are painted a dark red and there is gold writing on them, I wonder if these are more instructions on using the room but it is impossible to know. I throw my toilet paper into the basket with an odd feeling of guilt, even though I am doing exactly as instructed. I can sense my grandmother watching me, not an unfamiliar feeling.

I rinse my hands at the sink and pat my face, which is sweaty and swollen looking. I look like my sister. We look like my mother. I smile into the mirror and my sister smiles back.

I breathe deeply, a slight hesitation before opening the door.

'You can't put the paper in the toilet?'

'Nah. Old sewerage system. Can't even do a shit in some pubs. There's this one place that has a sieve in the bowl and a sign that says *You shit you pay*. They'll charge you, too.'

'That's crazy.'

She leans in close to me and I can smell her perfume, woody, musky, expensive probably. 'If anyone's afraid that China's going to take over the world,' she says, 'they'd better think again. No country can be a superpower till they get their sanitation under control.'

I laugh. She grins. She settles back in her seat and just as I feel myself relaxing she begins to ask about home.

'I visit Oma sometimes,' I tell her.

Her face is noncommittal. 'Does she even know you're there?'

'Yes. She does. She can't really speak.'

'Nice place?'

'Public health. Okay I suppose. They have a garden.'

'You were always a good girl.' She sucks down the last of her cocktail and turns towards the bar. She puts two fingers in the air, an impolite sign or just the number of cocktails she is ordering.

Isabel says, 'Coming up.'

'Becca the good sister.' And I don't know if she is being nasty or just stating a fact.

'Hard job,' I tell her. 'Someone's got to do it.'

'That's what Raphael says. And anyway, you do it with such style.'

The drinks arrive and I take a large sip of mine as she launches into a monologue about the other artists in the group exhibition. *Raphael says.* I want to wind her back, lay those two words out on the table as a valuer might lay out diamonds, holding them up to the light, hunting out imperfections with a magnifying glass. My mouth is sealed and I just nod and nod and when she says '—don't you think?' I can think of nothing to say to her at all.

'I'm pretty tired,' I say instead.

'First time overseas for you.'

And how does she know that? How does she know so much about me?

She downs the last of her cocktail. Mine is already empty.

'I want to pay my way when I'm here.'

She shrugs, 'I know how much you earn.'

'How? How do you know that?'

'We're sisters aren't we?' and she slides the money across the counter before I can protest any more.

It is nice riding in the dark. It is hot still, but the edge has worn off the day. A slight breeze lifts my hair away from my neck.

We turn a corner. There is a flash of light. Fire, flame. Some small wisp of brightness drifting skywards. I slow down to see a woman and a man squatting, they hold a match to something and it burns between their fingers, lifting off into the air. I glance behind me, the bike swaying, just a little snatch of fire drifting upwards and the couple watch it as it burns away to darkness. I look to my sister, a bright beacon, and in her wake I will not be lost.

Her flat is still tiny. We lock the bikes together in the courtyard and then we are inside where it seems I have nowhere to stand while she puts the kettle on and begins to make tea.

'It's really good to see you,' she says. 'I should have called you sooner. I've spent all this time thinking you probably wouldn't want to see me ever again and then here you are.'

I sink into one of the lounge chairs. My feet don't quite touch the ground and I would love to tuck them up under me but the chair is white and even in my socks I might mess it up somehow. She puts a cup of tea down on the table beside me. White with one. Like my grandmother, she knows almost everything about me; but not quite.

'There's only one bed.' She nods towards the staircase, so steep that it is almost a ladder. 'We'll have to be in the same bed. Is that a problem?'

'No.'

The tea is too strong. She used to know exactly how I like my tea. I suppose that was years ago. I hold the cup to my face and the steam curls up to my sweat-slicked skin. Our grandmother used to say that hot drinks on hot days cool you down.

'I could have bought an extra mattress…'

'No, it's okay. Same bed is fine.'

'I might have a shower first if that's okay.'

'Of course.'

'Really. It's great to have you here.'

'Thanks. It's good to be here. Honestly.'

She takes a step towards me and for a moment I think she might kiss me on the lips or hug me, or even stroke my hair.

Instead she takes the cup from my hands even though there is still an inch of dark hot liquid in the bottom of it.

In the doorway to the bathroom she stops and turns to me. 'Oh,' she says, 'don't rinse your toothbrush under the tap okay? It's easy to forget how toxic the water is.'

'Oh. I think I did that before.'

'Really?' she shrugs. 'Ah well.' And then she shuts the door behind her and I hear the sound of the shower turning on.

It is a long time before I can sleep. It is the heat of course but it is also Emily, lying so still it seems impossible that she is sleeping. I remember lying on my side and watching her, the still, stone statue of her, the sheer weight of her sleep. I am jittery like I used to be. I can't settle. I realise I am waiting. There is that whirlpool in the pit of my stomach. She smells clean, like hand cream, almond milk perhaps. My eyes are closed but she is there. I can feel her, the heat off her. I kick the sheets off my shoulder and sigh. Outside there is the sound of traffic, bells, car horns, a restless city standing vigil with me.

I wake to the feeling of her hand on my knee. I can't believe I managed to find sleep at all but now I am awake and the palm of her hand is touching my knee and my body is humming with the heat of it. I open my eyes but hers are closed. She is asleep of course. She has rolled over in her sleep and her hand has fallen onto my skin and she does not even know. I hold as still as I can. My leg is shaking a little. When she rolls the other way the loss of her touch is an unexpected disappointment.

Sick in Beijing

I am sick. I open my eyes and I know it instantly. I suppose it was something we ate, but I can hear my sister shuffling around in the next room and she sounds well enough. The bedside clock glows with the numbers 3:00. Early morning then, and Emily up and stretching canvases by the sound of it. A waft of oil paint and I think I might throw up.

I miss John, a brief stab in the chest, but now I have to get to the toilet and even the act of sitting up unsettles the world as if it were a boat. I cling to the edge of the bed, one hand on my stomach. I am seasick, but worse. I hurl myself at the door, but there are the tall stairs which might as well be a ladder and I turn and ease myself down them stair by painful stair. I am a balloon and there is too much helium inside me. I am floating and stretching and I am afraid that I might burst before I get to the bottom of the stairwell.

When I emerge from the bathroom my sister is standing in the lounge room with her hand on her hip. She almost glows with her own good health. She is wearing makeup. Her face is a flawless mask of powder and paint. Her hair is carefully pulled back and pinned. She is wearing a red tunic over black trousers. Red suits her. I suddenly see again the great beauty that she was. She smells of linseed oil and even this, one of my favourite smells, is making me want to vomit again.

'See? You washed your toothbrush under the tap.'

'I thought it might have been what we ate.'

'You can't touch the water. Don't open your mouth in the shower, don't let a drip of it remain in the bottom of your glass when you rinse it. You should boil the water before you wash the dishes.'

'Okay.'

'Breakfast?'

'It's 3am.'

She stares at me, sizing me up.

'Dry toast and tea? We're up anyway.'

'Maybe.'

She turns towards the tiny kitchenette, fills the kettle from the plastic drum of water and sets it on the stove. I am damp. My shirt is soaked in sweat. My skin is slick with it. I sink into one of her white couches and it is just like it always was, I am messing her place up, even my skin on her couch is causing damage. I remember the line stretching from one side of the room to the other, the chaos held back by a simple strip of duct tape like a force field. I am in her space now.

'You're not going to throw up on my couch are you?'

'I hope not.'

'Well don't.'

I stare at the bathroom door. I will launch myself towards it at the slightest indication. The smell of the bread toasting is a comfort. Maybe I am hungry. Maybe it will just be the one time and it is out of my system for good.

'Raphael says I should put a skull and cross bones on the tap so that you remember not to go near the water.'

'Emily…'

She brings me a plate, dry toast, and it does look good.

'Hmm?'

She sits cross-legged in the other couch and catches the crumbs on the plate raised under her chin.

'Thanks for the toast,' I tell her.

'I've got to go out.' She licks the butter off her fingers.

'It's dark outside.'

'Did that ever stop you and Raphael?'

I put my head in my hand. 'Emily. Can you hear yourself?'

She leaps forward and hits the plate from my hand. I flinch. The plate crashes to the tiles. Shards of it slide under the chairs. She stares at the pieces of crockery on the ground.

'Don't bother to thank me.' The door slams closed behind her and I hear her rattling the bicycles. She has taken nothing, no purse, no handbag.

It is dark outside but there is still the sound of traffic.

I am overcome by a wave of nausea and hold onto the arms of the lounge chair till it passes. In the bathroom the wall of the shower cubicle is a gaping hole with a frame of shattered glass. I wonder again what might have happened. How long has she been like this?

I find a dustpan and brush under the sink and tie the shards of plate in a plastic bag. I do remember. I suppose I will never be free from memory. I drag myself up the too-steep staircase, hand over hand, only realising when I have settled into bed, that I should have looked for a bucket.

There is a glass of water on my sister's side of the bed. I reach for it, sip. I put the glass down beside the packet of tablets. Clozapine. The tablets are in a blister pack with the days of the week beside each one. The packet is pristine. None of the little capsules have been popped. I shake one of the packets and hear the delicate rattle like a snake ready to leap up and bite me.

Van Gogh with his ear. Ian Fairweather with his raft. Emily Reich and her dirigible although I always thought it was supposed to be a balloon. All I know is that it didn't really fly.

I suppose it is the madness that lends her greatness. I suppose that she needs her madness now when she is getting ready for such a big exhibition. The memory of my own recent failure in the art world comes back at me suddenly like a splinter, forgotten, then knocked against a wall. I never read the review Emily was talking about but I can't see how it could have been so favourable.

I lie back on my side of the bed. I am exhausted and I can feel myself falling back into sleep. I look at the clock. 3.45. What does my sister do in Beijing at 3.45am? Opium dens? Cock fights, illegal gambling? None of these would be surprising.

Rain

My grandmother rarely listens to the radio. Natural disasters make her suddenly interested in the world outside the house.

There was another time, a flood, the road cut off and a warning that the town, which is on a flood plain, might be evacuated. My grandmother refused to be moved. She talked to our mother although my mother could not talk back. She talked and my mother began to smile as if she recognised the sound of our grandmother's voice and was pleased to be consulted. I listened as our grandmother came to the same idea again and again. We would not be evacuated. We would stand our ground. My grandmother dragged a ladder into the house and magically a trap door appeared in the ceiling that had never been there before. I followed her up into the loft. A hot crawl space and the sound of the rain like horses galloping across the roof.

Her torch lit up a horror show of cobwebs, broken toys, boxes labelled *books* and *papers* and *tax*. A furry arm protruded from a garbage bag. I scratched at the plastic till the hole was large enough to rescue the stuffed rabbit. A vague memory, the rabbit, clean and alert on a pink pillow. My pillow? My sister's? I put the rabbit under my arm and my grandmother tutted at me.

'Bec, drop it. That's full of dust mites.'

I dropped the rabbit and brushed the invisible mites from my clothes. My scalp began to itch, irritated by the idea.

'It's okay,' I said. 'I don't want it anyway.'

The lights from the torch swung in wild arcs into the far corners of the roof.

'What are you searching for?'

'Snakes,' she told me, and then she laughed. 'We won't want snakes up here if we have to sleep in the roof.'

'Why do we have to sleep in the roof?'

'Go back down, Bec,' my grandmother said in her speaking-to-the-dogs voice, but I was already balancing on the top step of the ladder. I am not especially frightened of snakes but the thought of them up there somewhere in the dark made me uneasy.

That last time when it flooded, I watched as she packed other people's paintings into wooden crates. One of the paintings was of a woman without clothes on. Oma rarely let us see the paintings because they were too precious to hold up in the light. Something about the woman's body made me uncomfortable, the sleepy abandoned pose, the slight parting of her fleshy legs, the way her breasts drooped heavy and low. I stared at the painting and began to feel a little upset in the stomach but also kind of warm and like I wanted to fall down sleeping too. The naked woman in the painting had that effect on me, like Dorothy walking through the field of poppies, barely able to hold up her head. I wanted to lie down in the same open-limbed way, cup one of my tiny breasts in my hand, just like the woman was doing.

Oma put the painting gently in its crate. She made me hold the plastic in place as she pushed the staple gun down hard, wrapping the paintings in a waterproof layer. It was not enough, of course. Even with the wooden crates and the plastic and storing them in the roof, they would still be ruined if the flood waters got up high enough. We would be ruined. Each one of these paintings was worth more than we could ever earn in all our lifetimes. *These are the most important things in the house* she told us, and I glanced towards our mother, standing at the window, staring out as if she were measuring the rain, counting the drops one by one. I wondered how I would protect Emily from the flood. I imagined pinning her down, wrapping her in plastic, storing her in the roof with the priceless paintings. I remember thinking that just this once my grandmother was completely wrong.

There is water up past our ankles. We are wearing our wet shoes and it doesn't matter that our bare shins are covered in mud. I put tea tree oil on my legs but it will be gone by now, washed away, the leeches will find me.

We walk till we reach the far end of our property. The ground has become a lake. There are no islands of grass here. There is just a knee-deep sea for us to wade in. I can feel the tug of the current at my feet. This part of our land is now a river. She stands in the shallows and clings to the fence for support. She whistles; we wait. He wouldn't be able to ford the river anyway. Still she listens, swinging slightly on the top rung of the fence.

I brace myself against it as my sister stoops and climbs through. Her raincoat catches briefly on a snag of barbed wire. She stands on the other side on the neighbour's land and looks back towards me.

'Shouldn't we go back?' I ask and she shakes her head.

Our house is a tiny brown rectangle amongst a tangle of trees. From the back step, with binoculars, you can see this fence. In the past I've used the binoculars to spy on Flame, watching him lean through the fence to tear at the longer grass on our side. It's impossible to tell if our grandmother is on the back step. Emily is waiting for me. Emily wants me to join her. She steps towards me and I flinch, but she touches the fence repeatedly. I watch her lips move as she counts. Fifteen touches and then she turns and looks away from me. I feel left out when she does this kind of thing, as if there is a game and no one has told me the rules.

I bend and step through the barbed fence and my coat doesn't rip. I don't fall. Nothing bad happens. I am standing outside our property in the bright light of day. I refuse to imagine what the punishment would be but I am certain that disobeying our grandmother by leaving our property in broad daylight is an unimaginable sin.

Emily says nothing, turns and continues her trudge. I have been here with Raphael, but in the darkness it seems different. In the daylight there is less difference between our side of the world and theirs. There is a small cluster of trees in the distance and Emily turns towards these. Horses like to rest under trees, particularly in this kind of thunderous rain.

The water is higher here. It is a creek, a fast-moving creek, I have to use my hands to move through it. The water is inside my yellow rain pants, they are ballooning with liquid, and the shock of cold wets my knickers. I have a sudden urge to urinate. No one would notice. I could pee right into the water. I am an adult now, I remind myself, trying to control the pain in my bladder.

Emily has forded the newly made creek. She shakes out her yellow pants and continues on without looking back. I scramble through the muddy water. A branch of a tree idles past with a dead native pigeon caught in its leaves. I slip on something and for a moment the water sweeps my feet out from under me. I regain my footing with difficulty.

I want to turn around. This place, the neighbour's property, makes me nervous. There will be locals here somewhere, that boy we met once, only now he will be a man, tall and broad and frightening. There are other people's houses surrounding us, country boys like our Oma described to us, drinking beer and swearing and shooting pigs. I turn and look back towards our house but it has disappeared over the ridge. If our grandmother were to look through binoculars she would see nothing.

I drag myself out of this new-formed river and trip up the ridge where my sister stands beside a tree. I am wet and don't want to be out here, I want us to go home. I climb up to the motionless statue that is my sister. I have a sudden urge to tug at her yellow rain jacket like I would have when I was much younger. I am wet and there are probably leeches all over me and I want to go home and so I touch the back of her jacket just lightly and I would beg her to turn around. I would beg her to come home with me but something in her face makes me pause.

The ridge is a bank. Beyond the bank is a river, a real one, a torrent, the kind you would whitewater-raft down in an adventure story. Emily is staring upstream to where the river becomes a sudden tangle of fallen trees. Foaming water churns past the blockage, sticks thump against each other, sucked under, thrown up again.

When we were little we used to play at steeplechases. I remember it in my bones. I remember the horses falling as if I had actually watched them fall. Eyes white with fear, teeth bared. I remember the pitiful shapes of the fallen and the dead, although I never really saw them fall at all.

They didn't look like this, fat and bobbing, barrel-chested. There wasn't this single hoof aimed skyward, these branches wrapped like a thorny skirt around chestnut flanks.

I imagine how the dry creekbed filled, new rain washing straight over the hardened earth. The mountains upstream and the tiny rivulets feeding it, gathering power, the sudden force of the water, the sheer volume of it following the old creekbed, a wall of water that could knock even a strong horse off his feet. Or maybe it was a slow swelling, finding its shape as Emily and I stood at the fence calling and calling and Flame did his best to swim across. Maybe it was an uprooted tree travelling slowly, its roots a net, a surprise ending. Hooves kicking out against the trip of branches, the white of his eyes bulging in surprise.

My sister's raincoat is slick under my fingers. I hold it tight but it is an inert thing. She doesn't turn or blink or breathe. I tug on her coat one more time and my fingers slip and then she turns and it is her face but it is not her face at all.

My sister's face is gone and this demon of fury and horror has taken her place. Perhaps if I had the right thing to say, to make the world good again it would be all right. But my sister stares and I find I can say nothing at all. I open my mouth, but there is only the rain coming in.

Dear B

An old man pedals a bicycle with a tray attached. There is a train of children following him, reaching out with chubby little hands to stroke and to touch. The tray is filled with bottles and cages and bowls. A guinea pig blinks through the bars, there are birds and little grass thatched cages on grass strings. In a shallow bowl a handful of tiny turtles climb over each other, little clawed legs struggling to gain purchase on the curved walls of their cell. A boy picks one up and shakes it towards his friend. She shrieks and claps and the old man spits onto the ground and shouts something that makes the boy set the turtle back in its glass entrapment. The children peel away but others join them. I watch as the entourage slowly winds its way between bikes and scooters, pedestrians and motorcycles till they are swallowed up by the crowd and disappear.

I wonder where my sister has gone. I wait at her place eating plain white bread, which it seems I am able to stomach without feeling too wretched. I make tea but pour that down the sink and replace it with water from the cooler in the kitchen.

I walk a little way, glance in shops. It should be easy enough to work out the prices of things but I am confused. In my head it seems that the hand-embroidered silk scarves are very cheap but then in the next shop a mass produced paper lantern seems to be not much less than the scarf. A printed T-shirt is four times the price of both of these things added together. I massage the side of my head, which has begun to throb.

Still no sister. There is nothing in the refrigerator except three bottles of Tsingtao beer and a can of tonic water. My stomach lurches when I think about food but it's been a while since the toast. The bed smells of sweat and faintly of tobacco. The vat of filtered water is almost empty and I draw down a small glass and sip it gingerly. The smell of cooking wafts in through the kitchen window, pungent Chinese spices. I breathe through my mouth, battling another wave of nausea.

Outside in the little alleyway leading to my sister's flat a neighbour has filled a plastic trough with water and put a small upturned bowl in the bottom. A turtle perches on it, a pet I suppose, although maybe it has been bought for a particular meal. Turtle soup, turtle dumplings. I sidestep the trough and find my way out to the street. A young man throws a ball to a pale-eyed husky pup, slinks back into the open door of a place called Bye Bye Disco. He falls into an overstuffed couch, picks up a piece of rope and dangles it towards the dog, letting it nip and leap and tug on the end.

There are no customers in this little bar, just the young man and a friend drinking gin and tonics. The friend lies across the couch looking as if he is dying of consumption. I manage a thin smile, but the young man glances in my direction briefly and turns back to the game with the puppy. A little further down the street another man is threading things onto bamboo skewers. There is already an array of pre-cooked delights to choose from. Scorpions and what look like centipedes, strips of meat, long snaky ribbons that might be thick noodles although why you would put a noodle on a stick and fry it is beyond me. I should eat, but even the smell of this food is enough to make the bile rise up into my throat.

The entry to the little café is down a step and past a little thrown-together pond. There are goldfish swimming through the tiny waterfall, another smaller turtle treading water, lifting itself up onto a shiny rock.

'*Ni hao.*' The girls at the counter are friendly. The window seat is free and I settle into it, rest my head in my hands. When the waitress delivers the menu I try not to look as if I might vomit on her.

'How are you today?' she asks. Her English is heavily accented but the words are recognisable.

'I've been better,' I tell her, and she nods.

'Very well thank you.' And there her English ends. Since my Mandarin has not even begun, I point at the photo of a glass of soda and she nods. I point at what looks like a piece of melon and she nods again. Fruit and water. At least this is what I hope I have ordered. She takes the menu away and I rest my cheek on my arm and gaze out the window to the busy street.

Across the road a door opens. I am distracted from my

low-level nausea for long enough to watch a tiny woman shuffle out onto the busy *hutong*.

It is hard to tell how old she is. Doll-like, slightly hunched, a face that could be seventy or a hundred. She looks from left to right and back again, seemingly a little dazed. I can just see an old gas stove behind her, a frypan balanced on one of the burners. This is her house. She stoops and drops a yellow plastic rubbish bag near the closest tree. She is wearing slippers, a housecoat, everything in shades of brown, but perhaps the housecoat was once green. It looks too warm for such a hot day. She shuffles across to the tree at the other side of her door, finds a scrap of paper with her toe and kicks it till it falls amongst the tree roots. A small act of civic pride that marks this as her street. Maybe she has lived here all her life, and what she must have seen in that time. The sudden social upheaval that was the cultural revolution, this new encroaching trudge of capitalism, the gentrification of her *hutong*. She checks her yellow plastic bag. Yes. It is still there. She turns and shuffles back inside and shuts the door behind her. The window into her world is closed. It is just a wall between two shops with no indication that anything lies behind it.

I clutch my soda water, sip gingerly. The bubbles settle my stomach. If I think about it too much I am overwhelmed by a wave of nausea but it is nice to be up and out and sitting quietly. I catch a waft from a nearby public toilet, a hint of shit and spice tinged with urine. I breathe through my mouth, take little sips of water. I open my book, flatten out the spine. The words blur into each other. I close it and slip it back into my handbag. Staring out the café window seems a lot less demanding at the moment. I watch some unusually well-dressed Chinese girls giggling together. They each have little white ears clipped into their uniform black bobs. One of them hops, makes cute little paws of her hands. Another tries to remove the ears, which seem to be sewn onto bobby pins, but the other girls slap at her hands, secure the ears more firmly. They skitter away, shrieking and pointing towards a dessert bar that has a huge queue of kids lined up outside it.

He is leaning on the tree with the yellow plastic bag at the base of it. It is unusual to see a western face, but not a complete surprise. A few other foreigners have been wandering down this famous *hutong* glancing at their *Lonely Planet China* or their *Top Ten Beijing*. But there is something familiar about this face. I feel myself beginning to smile, a greeting, my hand half-raised before I realise I don't know him at all. Not one of my students, he is too old, perhaps as old as I am, a middle-aged man with some grey coming, in a crumpled light cotton suit.

He taps a cigarette onto his palm. Camel unfiltered. I am struck by a wave of nostalgia. The taste of tobacco sharp on my tongue. Filthy habit, but I do remember it fondly. Learning to smoke. Smoking and kissing. I touch my front tooth with my finger and wish I hadn't, more germs for my stomach to battle. I wipe my lips on the back of my hand.

The man lights his cigarette, bends and tucks the dead matchstick into the yellow bag. He turns and looks directly at me and he smiles before slipping the packet of Camels into the top pocket of his jacket and walking off down the *hutong*.

I know him. I am certain I know him. I half stand. I could just say hello, see if he recognises me from somewhere. The idea of someone, something from home is so comforting. If he doesn't know me at least we could have a conversation in English. I settle back onto the chair. I watch his back disappear into the crowd. The door opposite opens once more and the old woman emerges, shuffles over to her yellow plastic bag, bends, picks it up by the handles, settles the dust and rubbish inside it, puts it back down and nudges it with her foot. She straightens and peers around at the crowd seeming both startled and hesitant. The changes. And how quickly things might change again. She shuffles back into her house and shuts the door.

I finish the last of my watermelon. The skin has been sliced and curled back on itself, delicate green fingers. A fancy wave. It is comforting to have something in my stomach. I feel a slight rush as from a drug, the sugars jangling in my bloodstream. I glance out of the window, hoping to see that ancient woman straightening her bag of dust again, and he is back. Leaning against her door. It is as if he knew I would be searching for the old lady and put himself in a place where he would be noticed. My psychiatrist would tell me to re-think that. I am not supposed to indulge my tendency to paranoia. So it is a coincidence then, but an odd one, that same familiar face, a name on the tip of my tongue.

I search through my wallet and find some notes to leave on the table, enough. I stand and move towards the door.

'*Xie xie.*'

'*Xie xie,*' the waitress says back to me. 'Bye bye.'

I dodge a gaggle of small children, a car, a bicycle. When I have made the small but fraught journey across the road the man is no longer anywhere in sight.

★

It is easier to ride than to walk. Just a quick lap of the *hutong*. I step up onto the rusty frame. The chain creaks, the tyres are sluggish. They are probably flat or else I am too heavy. Fat white girl on a bicycle. Still, the slight breeze that is generated by my body moving through the air is pleasant. A car beeps behind me and I pull over to a shop door, rest my foot on the stair. Nothing happens fast here; I am struck by the lack of road rage. Cars beep, bicycles chime but this is to warn the rest of the traffic, a little burst of care, not impatience.

I sway through the strolling throng, light headed. A fug of stench wafts from a *hutong* toilet. My guts turn, I breathe through my mouth. I will not be sick. To do so I would have to walk into that wall of stench to vomit into a vulva-shaped ceramic hole in the ground. I ride past as quickly as I can. Breathe in the slightly cleaner air of a Korean cold noodle restaurant. Another barrage of unfamiliar smells, but I am holding up well. When I see him I have regained my confidence. His hands are thrust into the pockets of his shorts, sweat under the arms of his T-shirt.

Raphael. I know it is Raphael. I also know that it can't be Raphael.

Shared Delusional Syndrome. Folie à deux. I know what was wrong with me. I have been diagnosed and there is a certain relief in having a name for your troubles. I am cured now. The madness belonged to Emily, and I borrowed it from her for a while but now I am sane. This cannot be Raphael but here, looking at him close up, there is no question. This is him, here, after all these years.

A gaggle of teenagers run in front of me pointing into the window of a shop and I am forced to step off the bike before I tumble off it. He has ducked into a shop. That is the only place he could go. I walk my bike slowly past the rows of windows. I know he will be here somewhere, but when I walk the length of the street I haven't seen him at all. I turn, and perhaps that is him, vanishing down another alleyway. I climb back on the bike and ride after him, past him, but it is not the same man. It is someone much older, not the man I saw moments ago. Not Raphael. Not my Raphael. Not Emily's Raphael at all.

I suppose this foray is too soon. I am not well. There are toilets on every street and alley in the *hutongs*. That stink of human shit, the steady reek of urine. I will have to use one now. There is no helping this. Inside, I breathe through my nose. There are little porcelain recesses in the floor but no partitions between them. Squat toilets, rows of them. No toilet paper anywhere and I will need toilet paper. In the corner there is a basket of soiled tissues. I have tissues in my pocket. There is no one else in the room. If I hurry I can be done with it before anyone comes in.

I ease my pants down and squat at the furthest porcelain bowl from the door. It is the closest I can come to hiding. Still, I find it difficult to concentrate on the task at hand. I am almost ready when an old woman shambles into the toilet block. She looks as old as my grandmother, perhaps older. She is small with a face wizened like a fallen apple. You can barely see her face through all the wrinkles. She is hunched almost in half and at first I imagine that her sight has gone because she shuffles over towards me. There are rows and rows of these toilet holes and yet she moves past them all and stands facing me where I am squatting. She lifts her skirt a little with one hand and then she lowers herself, rocking forward, backward, I imagine she might fall but when she is at her most precarious she reaches out with both of her hands and holds fast to my shoulders and makes the last of the crouch in this way.

I let her hold me. I close my eyes and clench my bowels despite the pain. I breathe through my mouth. When she is done she pushes herself up, using my shoulders. I keep my head bowed and my eyes closed and only open them when I hear her shuffling steps disappear out the entryway. And then I feel the embarrassing hot rush from my own bowels. It is some relief but I find that I am crying anyway. There is only a handful of days till the exhibition opening and then I will leave. I will go home and never accept an offer from Emily ever again.

I lean the bicycle against hers. It takes up all the courtyard. I have to sidestep the bikes to reach the door. There is something slipped under it, a letter. I recognise the handwriting because I have marked enough of his exam papers. He has tiny writing, the *g* is old fashioned, looping back on itself. He has a neat script and it is easy to read his name printed on the back.

I open the door and sit at the small table, rushing to open the envelope, tearing it, wrestling the paper out and onto the flat surface in front of me.

Inside John has written a short letter.

Dear B
I find that I am missing you very much. It is a shame you left exactly when you did. There was no time for a reconciliation. I have regrets. I think you do too. Classes are not the same without you, Old Paddy makes us do cut and paste like in kindergarten. Collage he calls it. What is this? The seventies?

Anyway, I walked past your place the other day and noticed that your jasmine was drooping. There has been no rain. I came back with a jug of water and now your jasmine and I have become great friends. She opened some flowers for me the other day. I enclose one here. I do hope the inclusion of this bud does not mean we have trouble with customs.

I hope you are enjoying your time with your sister. I hope you don't mind that I tracked down her current address. The internet is an amazing thing is it not?

I hope to see you on your return. I miss you greatly. I have already mentioned this but it is worth repeating.

Regards,

J

I fold the letter and put it in my pocket. I feel slightly better now. Still light-headed, still dizzy. Collage. The thought of it makes me smile, and the way he would say it, what is this? The seventies? He writes exactly as he speaks. Another one of his endearing qualities. I take the letter out of my pocket again. I read. His voice in my head. His clear, unique voice. I want him to be here. I want him to be sitting at the table with me, joking, lightening the mood. His cheerfulness protects me. I hold the letter to my nose. Sniff the paper. There is no trace of the scent of him at all. It smells like paper and perhaps a hint of dust, and I am strangely disappointed.

Incantation

We sit at the table and wait for Emily. Oma has her binoculars by her plate. She stands once again and moves to the window. She stares out into the growing dark. There is nothing to see. The rain alone would be enough to obscure the fenceline. Our mother seems agitated. She stands, and Oma grabs at her elbow, pushes her roughly back down to her seat. She opens the pot steaming on the stove and there is a deep rich smell of cardamon, basil, onions. She dips the ladle and scoops up the vegetable stew and slops it onto the plate in front of mother, who picks up the spoon and stares at it as if she has never seen one before.

I know how she feels. Dinner is ridiculous. Emily is still outside somewhere in the dark and here we are sitting down as if everything is ordinary. I chew at a mouthful of the stuff. Everything tastes like this, the same spices every night, the same vegetables, pumpkin, carrot, celery. I put my spoon back on my plate and chew until there is nothing I can do but swallow. The food is all in a lump. I feel it travelling too slowly down my oesophagus. I feel it stopping, swallow several times in an attempt to get it down. Just this one mouthful is a struggle. I look at the pile still on my plate. I glance out the window. It is almost completely dark. There is no moon. Rain is a blanket between us and the sky.

'May I be excused for a moment Oma?'

She frowns. She was already frowning, her head tipped in the direction of the window as if waiting for something to appear in it, some spectre of my sister, pressing her hands against the glass.

'Why?'

'To use the bathroom?'

I do not need to use the bathroom, but I need a moment to myself before I attempt another spoonful of food.

She nods. Pushes her own food around on her plate as if the whole pot is spoiled. I shove my chair back and walk down the corridor to the bathroom. It feels like the house is a boat. I touch the wall lightly with my fingers for balance. The world is on a tilt but I am not sure which way it is tilting. It feels like the brushing of my fingertips against the faded paint is the only thing keeping me upright. The close walls of the toilet are a relief. I can lean one way and the cool wall is there to meet my shoulder. The other side is equally close, and if I lean forward far enough I feel the top of my head brush comfortingly against the door. I have been alone with a boy and Flame is dead and my sister is missing and nothing will ever be the same again.

I lean far enough forward to push the top of my skull against the door. I reach out with my elbows and press against the walls. Blood thuds in my head. Blood rushes to my face. I feel dizzy but there is an odd calmness in this feeling of suspended motion. Perhaps I can just sit here and do nothing for a while.

John and Raphael

When Emily does not return I wander back to the little café down the road. The waitress seems to remember me, although perhaps she is just over-friendly to any middle-aged western woman. I suppose we all look kind of the same.

I have his number on my phone. The phone itself is dutifully unlocked for overseas calls. *If you need me for anything.* Ed raised an eyebrow. *Go, Bec. Go. The university won't fall down without you.*

It is a simple thing to call his number, adding the appropriate prefix. I could ask him about the jasmine.

I dial and the ring tone is unfamiliar, a reminder of the distance between us. Even his voice seems far away, shrouded in static. It reminds me of the voice I dug out of the silence between the disconnected tones. It reminds me of Raphael. John is real, I remind myself. Raphael is not.

'Hey.'

And I say, 'Hi.' There seems to be a delay, but when his voice comes it is a sweet solid thing.

'Nee how,' he says. 'That's hello isn't it?'

'I think so.'

'I've been practising in case you decided to call me. Invite me to run away with you to China. I assume that's why you're calling me now?'

'Sure it is,' I tell him. And then, 'Actually I'm just checking on my jasmine.'

'Oh.' The delay is thick with all the miles between us. 'Really?'

'Maybe. I just got your letter.'

'I like letters. Don't you? Better than emails, except you have to wait a while.'

'Unless you send them priority post.'

'Yeah. It is kind of expensive but if I sent it regular mail you would be home before it arrived.'

'It was a nice touch. Despite the expense. Thank you.'

'My plane ticket will be more expensive. I might have to borrow some money from my mother.'

'Well, don't go borrowing it just yet.'

'That's a shame. I was hoping this would turn out to be that call. I've been poised for it, you could say.' I smile. This banter is normal. John is normal. This is the world I have come from and the one that I will return to afterwards.

'My sister's a bit crazy,' I tell him.

'Oh really? Emily Reich is crazy? You should tell the media about that. Stop the presses.'

'Yeah, okay.'

'Your sister is a schizophrenic, Bec.'

'I know.'

'So does everyone. *Women's Weekly* knows that, Channel Nine

News. Basically everyone in the western world knows that. Maybe half of China by now.'

'I suppose I'd forgotten.'

'Are you okay though? She hasn't hurt you?'

'No. She hasn't.'

'Cause I am not joking. My mum will be happy to buy me a ticket. I can be there in twenty-four hours—except waiting for the visa. God, how long did that take? Ages.'

'I'm fine.'

'It's no problem. I would love to come to China.'

'So you can see Emily Reich?'

'No,' and then a little pause. I can hear him breathing, a real live person breathing. 'To see you actually.'

My turn to pause, my turn to breathe into the phone. His turn to listen to my breath grow heavy with worry.

'John.'

'Yes.'

'Did you have an imaginary friend as a kid? Someone you really believed in?'

'No. But I jumped off the roof of a car once because I thought I could fly.'

'What happened?'

'I fell down.'

'Did you hurt yourself?'

'Of course I did. Bec, is there something wrong? Because if Emily hurts you I am going to come over and kill her. And then I'll steal all her paintings and flog them off on the black market and be really rich and marry you and live happily ever after.'

I should be laughing; would be if it wasn't for Raphael.

Raphael is all grown up now. He is a flesh and blood man settling down on the chair across from me.

'Hello?'

Too long a pause this time I suppose, but I open my mouth to reassure John and find that I am lost for words.

'Bec?'

'John.' A thin sound summoned from the sudden void in my chest.

'Seriously, I am hours away. Should I hit Mum up? She'll be so cool with it. If I tell her I have a girlfriend she'll mortgage her house for joy.'

'No, John. It's fine. I'll call you later.'

'You better.'

'I will.'

'Bec?'

Raphael reaches out a hand and touches mine. His hand is warm and real. John's voice is a little distant thing on the end of a bad line, barely audible at all as he tells me, 'I love you Bec. I really do. I miss you a lot.'

'Okay,' I say, and then, hurriedly, 'Bye.'

Raphael is here at the table with me. He turns and with his free hand, the one that isn't slipping his fingers between mine, he waves to a waitress. She sees him. She can see him. Raphael speaks to her in Mandarin and she nods.

'She can see you.'

He grins. 'Of course. I'm not invisible.'

He holds my fingers between both of his hands. He strokes the inside of my palm.

'I missed you Bec,' he says.

'But you aren't real.'

'Aren't I?'

The waitress puts two glasses on the table. I watch as he takes money out of his pocket, places it in her hand. He says something to her and she laughs. I look down to where the glasses are sweating on the table. I can smell gin. My stomach twists against itself. 'You are an illusion,' I tell him when the waitress is gone. 'You are imaginary.'

He shrugs.

I put my hands over my eyes and begin to count down from twenty. I know how to do this, but I haven't done it for years.

'What if I'm not imaginary? Isn't there even some potential for doubt?'

'Seventeen, sixteen.'

'What if I followed Emily here to China? Have been following her since that night in the barn?'

'Eight, seven.'

I keep my eyes closed and my hands over my ears till the sequence of numbers is complete. He is a product of my own doubt. I must be strong in the knowledge that he will have disappeared. I am cured. I know what is real and what is imagined.

He is gone, of course, but his glass is still there on the table. I pick it up and turn it in my hand. A lip print on the glass. I wonder how I managed to magic that up. Did I drink from both glasses? Am I so hell bent on this self-deception?

When the waitress passes I hold my hand up and she pauses, smiles, hurries to my table.

'Hello, how are you today?' She is sweet and bright and pretty. John would like her, I suspect.

'Did you see the man who was here?'

She seems concerned. Her brow furrows.

'You like to order?'

'No. Did you see a man here with me?'

'I am sorry.'

I point to the other glass, the lip print, the water sweating down the side and pooling at the base.

'Man,' I say, miming a beard although Raphael was clean shaven.

'I am sorry,' she says, and I nod.

'Drink?' she asks. I shake my head. Two drinks are more than enough for me. I sip at his glass, Raphael's glass, although it isn't his glass at all. I expect the alcohol will make me feel worse, but the gin settles quietly into my body. A slight numbness. A pleasant relief.

My phone buzzes and for a moment I know that it will be Raphael. It is John, of course. I click through to the message. *I just said 'I love you', in case you missed it. Don't know what I expected to happen. An earthquake? The end of the world? Instead it feels normal. Ordinary. Because it is true I suppose. You don't have to love me back, by the way. Just thought you should know.—PS It took me 8.5 mins to compose this text message—should have taken 30 secs.*

Sweet John. I close my fingers over the phone. It feels hot in my hand. I finish the last of Raphael's drink and push the glass away from me. I clutch the phone closer to my chest and the heat of it is comforting as I start to drink the second glass of gin.

Confessions

I crawl into bed and drag the thin sheet up over my head. The heat hasn't let up. I scratch at my ankle. There are red welts there, some fungal infection from the sweat trapped under my sock. I am tired of waiting for my sister to return. Tomorrow I will find my own way to Tiananmen Square, the Summer Palace, the Forbidden City. Even if I am ill I will find my way there slowly. Stopping when I need to. I will take the bicycle. I have three more days in Beijing and then I will have to return home.

I turn over onto my side, shift again, there is no breeze and it's impossible to settle. The sheets are already soaked in sweat. There will be no sleep. I feel the rough carpet under my feet. I open her top drawer. Her clothes are neatly folded, they smell lightly of lavender. I am ambushed by an odd sense of longing and, surprisingly, a sudden urge to paint.

Her studio is the only other room in the house. The smell seeps out above the closed door and when I turn the light on in the hall I can see that there is no wall above it, just a rent in the wall, an odd rough-edged space. It is as if she tore that part of the wall free with a hammer and perhaps she did. The paintings she has made for me seem too large to fit through an ordinary doorway. I can imagine Emily tearing the plasterboard free with her bare hands. Strange to find the door open. Our grandmother used to lock her studio when she left it and somehow I expected Emily would do the same.

Linseed oil, turps, paint. This is where I come from. The smell of the womb. If you cut a vein our blood would spill out alizarin crimson, cobalt blue. The colours of our tiny cloistered world. There are lines on the walls, dry paint where paintings were leaning against them until recently. When she was a child my sister would never spill out over the edges of a work. In this way she has become more like me. I trace a damp umber line, rubbing the pigment between my fingers. My own studio is similarly scarred by lines of errant paint.

There are stretched canvases resting in a bundle. Pristine, primed. I wonder if she still stretches them herself. *Good craft right from the beginning.* I touch the smartly stapled edge of the fabric, the stiff sealed surface. The work of an expert. My sister's work.

The brushes have been carefully cleaned and oiled and wrapped in a slightly damp tea towel. I unwrap them and bring the tips of the bundle to my nose. So beautifully soft. Softer than the brushes I can afford. Only the best. The paints are carefully sealed and ordered in their box, from the deepest colours, black, blues, browns, to the lightest whites.

I uncap a deep rich brown and squeeze a worm of it onto the palette she has left there, resting on the table with the rest of her equipment. I take a canvas and turn it and rest it against the wall.

I sit, cross-legged as I used to sit when I was a child. I feel the shift of focus in my eyes, my vision switching from the room to a place somewhere near infinity. I take a deep breath heady with the scent of colour. And I start to paint.

My hands smell of oil. I hold my fingers to my nose and the smell is calming, almost as pleasant as a lullaby. The scent of viridian— a day inching towards evening after rain—cadmium red—the picked clean salt-bone scent of some remnant of sea life. His hair is bleached blonde like a skeleton plucked from the ocean. His eyes are like algae. I let my eyes re-focus on the canvas and there he is, Raphael. The painting is nowhere near complete, but the face is particularly well realised, the eyes. The eyes are exactly right.

'You haven't captured the line of my jaw.'

He is there behind me. He is a shadow at first, a lean, a sharp jut of shoulder. He steps forward into the light from the lamp and there are the eyes from my painting. I have a creeping feeling that if I turn around now the canvas will be blank, just a smudge of background colour and a white space in the shape of a person. He is here in person. I am struck again by how physical he is. The air moves when he does, there is a stirring when he raises his arm and points. I remember how his lips felt against mine. The physical representation of a shared madness, a folie à deux.

'You are not real.' This is the mantra. I have learned it by heart. I now know what I must say, *If he ever comes back, close your eyes and tell him he is not real. He is your sister's imaginary friend. Count back from twenty. He will disappear.*

'You are imaginary,' I tell him, and then: 'He is imaginary.'

Because there is no Raphael to listen to my strange exorcism. I close my eyes. I start to count. I am grown up now. I am sane. I don't need to see her imaginary friends. I continue the count, steady, sure.

He shifts, but I can still feel his weight in the room, the length and breadth of him. A person sharing this space. I can smell him when he steps closer. He smells like the paint still wet on the canvas; I open my eyes quickly to glance back at it. He looks so real but when I turn and look at the phantom in the room it is not the same person. His jaw is different, softer, rounder. The eyes are the same but the hair is darker. I close my eyes once more and continue the count. Nine, eight, seven, I feel his hand on my cheek, his lips soft against my own. An imaginary kiss and imaginary chill when the lips pull away from mine and I say, 'four, three, two.'

I have run out of numbers. I open my eyes, blink in the half-light. He is still here, staring, watching too intently. I see now that his eyes are different from the eyes in my painting. There is a harshness to them, a tired cynicism. This is Emily's Raphael, not mine. Except it is not Raphael. I notice the downward curl of one side of his lip. Her lip.

'Emily?'

'Emily? She's off somewhere doing something, whatever she has planned for her terribly important exhibition. She is so boring, Bec. She paints and paints and paints…'

'Emily.'

'We have time,' she says. 'Emily won't be back for ages. I've missed you, Bec. I've never forgotten you.' She steps closer again and she would kiss me but I press my hand against her collarbone.

She is wearing a crushed velvet suit, boyish, but she is not a boy. If I let my hand drop she would step forward and kiss me again. I feel that old excitement, the kind of shivery anticipation that I haven't felt for all these years. I remember the kisses, and more, I remember more. My cheeks flare red, I can feel my skin burning. I turn towards the canvas. The man that is painted there has my sister's eyes, her mouth, her incredulous expression.

'Emily,' I say and the name conjures her. She frowns. She tilts her head. She becomes more herself. 'Emily. Hey. Em.'

'Don't call her,' she says, in her low and Raphael-like rumble of a voice. 'Emily never wanted you here. I made Emily call you, Bec. Don't call her back. I missed you. I love you.'

I take her shoulders and I shake her. I call her name and she looks around startled as if she is afraid that she might hear me and slip back into her body. She shrugs me off and trips backwards.

'Emily. It's okay, it's okay. Don't go.'

But she is scrambling away from me, 'You've spoiled it.' Her voice is a deep and frightened growl. 'Emily's heard you. Emily's coming.' And then she is gone.

Façade

I am careful to hold my skirt back, away from the paint. The painting is half done, and I suppose that's how it will stay. I settle her painting beside it. Mine is a smaller canvas. Hers is more grand. Her Raphael looks nothing like mine, I can see the differences in the light of the day. Her painting technique is similar to mine, but John was right: we are only similar painters. Not the same. My brush strokes are more visible. My expression more vague. Her Raphael has the corner of his mouth raised in a half-smile. It is the kind of expression that Emily herself might wear, sitting with the other artists in the restaurant, turning one corner of her mouth up in what is almost a sneer. Raphael has Emily's smile in her painting of him, but in mine he is just a sweet, tired man of my own age with eyes like my sister's, which are also like mine. There is a difference in the way we treat light. Even in this reproduction of Emily's style you can see my hand. The glow is gentler despite the directional brightness. It is easy to see which is her painting and which is not.

I finish zipping the dress up, walk out of the studio and enter Emily's bedroom. She doesn't meet my eyes. She having trouble with the buttons on her dress but when I step towards her she flinches away.

'It's okay,' she says, 'I've got it,' and continues to struggle with the fastenings.

I sit on the edge of her bed and fold my hands into my lap.

'It's my birthday today,' I tell her and she turns back towards me and this time her smile is even and genuine.

'Yes,' she says. 'Yes, I know.'

Galleria Continua

I can hear my mother pacing. I have never heard sounds from her room after dark. I always imagine she lies carefully, her bedside light switched off and her internal light similarly extinguished. She falls quickly into that drugged sleep, the sleep of the dead. It bothers me to hear her pacing like this.

The windows are locked. When I heard my grandmother moving from one window to the next, rattling her keys, I felt the panic rising in my chest. The windows are locked and my sister is outside.

It is impossible to lie down and sleep. I close my eyes anyway. His hair is sandy at the tips. His face is chiselled. His smile is lopsided. I picture every detail I can remember. I feel the creep of his fingers up and under my skirt. If I can capture him exactly he will be summoned. Raphael. I picture his name on Emily's lips. I feel a slight breeze and I open my eyes, expectant. The room is empty.

I am the good girl. I am here, safe in the warm house. Outside it is dark and the rain is a constant petulant complaint. The ground will be a swampy mess of puddles and mud. Somewhere outside my sister, the bad sister, is alone and sad and abandoned.

There is a longish drop but the mud is soft and my knees sink into it. I walk away from the house and the rain is like a thick cloud around me. The sound of it swallows the world. It makes me silent and invisible. I turn to look at our house and there is the shock of a face at the window. Mother's window. Our mother, staring vacantly out into the dark. For a moment it seems that she is looking straight at me.

I trip over a tree root. I hiss and wiggle my toe in my mud-covered shoe. When I look back towards the house the window is empty.

I find the fence, but in the wet dark, it is impossible to see. When I turn back the way I have come, it seems there is no house at all. The rain is a solid heavy curtain around me, thudding against my skin. The water has the weight of fists, a rough drubbing on my shoulders. The water runs down my chest and pools in my pants. This is my last pair of dry shoes. Even my boots are damp on the inside. For some reason the fact that all my shoes are wet has a certain finality to it. I must find my sister or there will be no dry shoes. It is so dark now I cannot even see my hands on the wire. I slide them; shuffle crablike through puddles up to my knees. Without the fence to guide me I would be lost.

My thigh bumps up against something before I can see it. I pause. A branch, foliage. It is impossible to see anything and the sound of the rain is like the roar at a sports stadium.

'Emily?'

My voice lost to the force of it.

'Emily? Raphael?'

It seems childish to be saying his name out loud. It feels fake, like a kids' game. My sister and I used to play a game where you call the pony and she gallops a little towards you till you turn around suddenly hoping to catch the movement of her hooves. If the pony is quick she will be frozen like a statue when you turn around. Calling Raphael now feels like I am calling the pony, but each time I open my eyes the world is frozen and there is no movement to be seen. No Raphael, no Emily, no sign of any pony at all.

Beijing is like Brisbane. There is certainly the same kind of oppressive heat that we have back home. My fingers, slick with sweat, fumble the champagne glass. There are some Chinese people in the crowd but it seems that every Australian expat in the country has gathered in the art district tonight. Remembering my own exhibition a handful of weeks ago, I am nervous, mostly for myself. Emily will be perfectly fine. Emily is always fine in her own crazy way.

We have spent the day together. She seemed relaxed. She seemed to know who she was. We hired a tour guide at the Forbidden City and the woman made us laugh with her frantic tracts of history learned by rote and her habit of appropriating my camera to take photographs at particular 'scenic' parts of the tour. *Smile cheese cheese cheese cheese* she said before every photograph, then hurried us forward. *Quickly, quickly. Plenty see. Hurry.* Emily could have spoken to her in Mandarin but she chose to remain silent, enjoying the theatre. In the end we escaped, ditching the guide before the tour was over. She had been paid. She wouldn't mind too much. We hid in a gorgeous ancient garden and Emily took my hand in hers and held it. It was my chance. I could have mentioned what had happened in the night but it was too nice a moment to spoil.

We lay in the same bed. Emily and I, side by side. I felt well, at last, and wondered about my nights with Raphael which must have been nights with Emily. What terrible things we did. How cleverly we hid this from ourselves. I turned towards her, letting my hand rest against the small of her back, wondering. She shuffled carefully away.

I dreamed of a storm, hailstones thundering down to smash on the ground. A pack of dogs were pressed up against my legs and one or another of the animals would take its turn to startle and run out into the thick of it. Hailstones like bricks, the potential for carnage, a mad dash to rescue the shaking little body of a whippet, crouching under cover as the hailstones rained down, each one bigger and louder, a hailstone the size of a cow. Dogs, running and howling and then it was too dangerous to run out and save them. Then the damage began in earnest.

Emily was standing, staring at me tangled in the sheets. I woke to the fear and the excitement. Fear of the storm, excitement because my sister was standing at the side of my bed and anything would be possible.

'Raphael?' I asked her in a whisper.

'It's Emily,' she said. 'You're just having a bad dream.'

The art district seems like a city within a city. The place is a warren of little streets and alleys. We walked past a square the size of a city block where a hundred bronze dogs snarled and threatened a lone warrior, caught forever in the moment before his death. Beyond this the galleries are lined up one beside the other. If you tried to visit them all you might take a year to complete the task.

The Galleria Continua is flanked by a pair of metal doors and the invited guests spill out onto the street where the waiters slink between them with their precarious trays. It is not a huge space, a spiral of stairs moves the crowd between one level and the next.

Emily has been given the ground floor, the biggest space. The other artists have their places on the floors above because the crowd is here to see Emily Reich. That is clear from the way their heads turn as she passes. She is the icing on this cake. The crowd parts as she passes, chasing a waiter across the room to pluck another glass from his tray. I have drunk too much but she has had more, and I am worried for her.

The black dress is tight at my breasts. It is strapless and I have a wrap, which I pull across the meat of my arms. I am, as always, too corporeal. My sister, is, as always, hard to grasp, impossible to figure out. I am flesh and she is nothing more than smoke.

These people are glamorous. Young, most of them, a few older men, grey haired and besuited. A thin, flamboyant woman with a shocking bob of red hair and an Australian accent laughs loud as a bell, joyously commanding the attention of the room. I suppose she is older than I am but she is gorgeous in a little drop of black crochet, a flash of garish tights beneath it. A handsome young Chinese man bends to whisper something in her ear. I notice the way his fingers ease into the small of her back, a tiny gesture of intimacy. He is perhaps half her age. I miss John, suddenly, acutely. This woman is a wild and exotic flower and she captures the arm of a waiter and whisks a glass from his tray. So many beautiful people. I shrink into my black dress, aware that my shoulders are hunched, sipping furtively from a champagne flute.

Emily is incandescent. She moves easily. I watch her working the room. She has a strange slightly overwound energy. She sweeps from one conversation to another, barely pausing to join in. She is wearing peacock blue nipped in at the waist, making her seem slimmer than she is. The silk is so fine that it fans behind her like a captured stream when she walks. I am proud of her and in one breath slightly apprehensive as she catches my eye across the room. Emily stops as if she is an appliance that has been turned off for a second. The smile disappears, the dress flutters to stillness around her abruptly immobile body. The loss of energy is only momentary but I have seen it, and when she turns, the smile flashing back to illuminate her whole face, it leaves me with a creeping unease that I can't shake.

There is a clinking, someone tapping a spoon against a glass. Speeches. Of course there will be speeches.

I cannot summon Raphael. I am exhausted from trying. It is cold and it is wet and my teeth make a clattering sound which reminds me of skeletons and that in turn reminds me of Flame's legs kicked and frozen stamping towards the moon. There is a sound, a rustling. For a moment it sounds human, footsteps. I am caught between fear and relief. What if it is Emily? I hold my breath expecting that she will slip under the bushes and snuggle here out of the rain, but the sound has stopped if it was ever there, a wallaby hopping away through the rain, or a snake searching for higher ground. Our property is all just muddy hills and new-formed lakes. I wrap my wet jumper around my shoulders although it is crazy to think that this will do anything to keep me warm. I imagine the leeches catching in my hair, raining down onto my back. I shudder, but push out into the weather. The rain is so heavy that I can't see anything at all. Emily could be standing a metre away and I would miss her.

I pull the wire of the fence down and step through. The barbs catch on my shirt, tearing the fabric. It doesn't matter. I will be in trouble anyway, a mountain of misdemeanours, one more will not bring Oma's wrath down with any more ferocity.

There is a sudden break in the clouds and a fragment of starry sky opens up above. The moon leaks through like the finger of god and touches the building in the distance, a light glance on the roof before the clouds move back, eating the light. Still, I saw the building, and I head towards it. Perhaps my sister saw it too. Perhaps she made her way to the only dry place in a big wet field. I move slowly and cautiously. The landscape here is unfamiliar. There are divots and small shrubs, things to trip on, places to slip against. I fall more than once and I am sure I have taken the skin off one knee.

It is a long way away. I am not certain how long, but it seems to take hours. I feel the damp flap as the rubber on the bottom of my shoe comes loose. It slows me down but I struggle on.

I can smell the barn before I see it. It is the smell of hay and horses. I feel tears spring to my eyes and I see his mouth, teeth bared, belly bloating and I walk faster, trying to outpace the memory.

The door is unlocked. I suppose there is no need to lock a barn. What is there to steal except horses? Maybe there is value in stolen horses, but you would think every horse is well known in a small town. Of course I am not certain of this.

There are two horses stabled here. One of them is white and has his mane braided neatly in a rather stupid mat of interwoven plaits. The other is a chestnut horse, big and strong with a dark twitch of a tail. I have never seen these horses before. The barn itself is small and smells of animals and hay. I remember the smell of Flame, my nose pressed into his flank as I hauled myself up and over, the smell of Raphael, pungent, sweaty, and slightly familiar, a sweet human musk.

It is so dry and clean in the barn. Fresh straw a vague pale sheen on the floor. It is dark, a building without windows. The clouds part for the second time tonight and there are thin slivers of moonlight squeezing between the boards and turning the horses into zebras. The sound of them is loud and close. I am shivering. My face itches. I can feel the leeches on the back of my neck although it is probably just my imagination.

The little white horse shifts noisily, nudging the side of his stall and I flinch. There is movement. Something pale. I glimpse it just as the moonlight disappears. Still, something scampered, large, the size of a dog perhaps. The size of a young girl.

'Emily?'

I hear the rustle of something moving, furtive, a slow creep.

'Raphael?'

The horses stamp and snort. They are unsettled.

'Emily? Come on, you're scaring me.'

Something shifts over there in the dark. I back away. There is a hot flank behind me. The horse stamps and snorts and it is a huge thing, I am small beside it, I turn and dart away from the thud of hooves against the wooden floor.

Something pale in the dark, limbs, legs, arms, a body, naked but for the mud. Hay catching in her hair like blonde spikes, for a moment I think it might be Raphael. I call out his name and she runs forward out of the dark, breasts bouncing awfully, the shock of her nakedness as she grabs for me, throwing me back and downward. We are tumbling. There are hooves near my head.

'Emily!' a thin shriek of a voice but the air has been knocked from me and then there is something in my mouth, something tugged hard, forcing my lips apart making it impossible for me to call out at all.

Galleria Continua is all about a desire for continuity between ages, the aspiration to have a part in writing the history of the present, a history that is sensitive to contemporary creative practices, which cherishes the link between past and future, differences and similarities, individuals and geographies.

I read the mission statement on the wall for the fifth time.

'Blah blah blah blah blah.' She is suddenly there with her face in my ear. I can smell her perfume, strong and spicy. She begins to read what I imagine is the Chinese translation underneath the printed English. The sounds seem so strange, these Chinese words and I am again struck by how quickly she has learned so much of a new language. I smile and turn but she is already a blur of watery blue heading off and away into the circle of her own art.

Her canvases are huge. They sit in stately observance. The figures in the portraits are each in formal Chinese robes, their hands balanced calmly on their knees. The robes are wonderfully executed and at this size it is possible to see every stitch in the

carefully painted silk embroidery. I recognise the genetic similarities in our style as if her paintings and mine are blood relatives.
In this series of portraits the movement comes from the faces, not
human faces but horses' heads. Some of the horses are staring
straight into the crowd, their wide frightened eyes following the
observer. Some of them are just a blur as if the horse was tossing
its head manically back and forth. One is a snarl and a lunge and
it seems so real, such a moment captured in time, that most of the
audience leave a little distance between themselves and the canvas
when they pass it as if the creature might lunge out and bite a
passer-by.

The images are unsettling in their realism, the hem of each of
the costumes is beginning to smoulder or catch fire. The stillest of
the horse-head men has a tiny lick of smoke creeping out from
the cuff of his crimson pants. The wildest blur of a horse-girl has
a lick of flame climbing up her leg and into the skirt hanging from
her lap. The human bodies do not demonstrate any kind of distress.
It is only in the wildly turning heads that we see the panic.

I recognise the feeling Emily has captured in these portraits.
The idea that you can be perfectly still and yet inside you can be
spurred to galloping. I am sure this can't be a feeling that only
Emily and I share, and I notice how quiet the crowd become
when they pass the most panicked of the portraits. As if they
themselves have become the human parts of the paintings, leaving
only a faint distress lining the corners of their mouths to prove
that they have been captured by this kind of claustrophobic
unease at all.

There are nine portraits. Three on each of the available walls.
Of course the paintings are not the only part of the exhibition.

It would be unlike Emily to let an audience off so easily.

She is drunk when she steps up on the rostrum. She is surrounded of course by the carcasses. A full one, its head lolling downward towards the audience, its feet tied in a pose reminiscent of David Cerny's *St Wenceslas Riding a Dead Horse* only in this instance the saint is conspicuously missing. Beside Emily is a hind leg suspended by the hoof. A hunk of flank spins in front of her so that I am forced to step to one side to see her.

'Meat,' she says in response to the inevitable question. 'Carcasses, prime cuts, cadavers.'

'Yes,' says the young British man who has asked her the question. 'But why?'

She stares at him then with an expression I am familiar with. Confusion, sudden awareness, uneasiness. She looks at him as if he has been transformed into a gibbering lunatic.

'He told me to do it,' she says.

I step forward. It is terrible to see my sister looking so lost and confused.

'Who do you mean?'

'Raphael.'

'Who's Raphael?

She blinks.

'Ms Reich, you haven't provided us with notes. The other artists have prepared a dossier. Can you explain why not? Is there some reason for this?'

She looks around, peering, as if searching for Raphael in the crowd. She finds me there instead and takes a step towards me, hovering at the edge of the podium. One more shuffle forward and she will fall off.

Emily points to me with her open palm, a ringmaster, directing the audience towards the main attraction, conjuring me out of the crowd. I am suddenly visible. I am stared at. 'My sister,' she says and people respond with a scatter of tentative applause. 'My sister, Rebecca Reich. Today is her birthday.'

And then she steps down and walks towards me and puts her arm around my shoulder.

Here, in the barn, I realise this is not a game. I am frightened of the horses. I am frightened of the neighbours who might find us here. I am frightened of my grandmother who might see that I am gone. I am frightened of Emily. Most of all I am frightened of Emily.

She ties the scarf around my head, pulling it tight so that it hurts my lips and I feel like I might choke. She has let the horses out of their stalls. I can feel them brush against my hip. She takes hold of my cold, soaked jumper and tugs it up and over my head. She grips my dress and although I struggle away from her, run for the door, she brings me down. I thump to the straw and my ribs ache at the impact. She is sitting on my thighs and she struggles the dress up and over my head. I would cry if I could, but my mouth is stuffed full of cotton and she is rolling me over, gazing down at me with a terrible intensity. I hold my arms tight into my body, my elbow pressing against my chest. I don't want her to see me this way, she takes my hands and forces my arms wide as though I am a butterfly pinned and waiting for death.

She is holding something. I see now that it is a hairbrush. I recognise it from somewhere. It is old and the bristles are white and there is a purple rose on the back of it. I must have seen it on our mother's dresser. She pulls it roughly through my hair and I try to scream. It hurts. My eyes water. I groan but there is no room for sound to come out.

Emily brushes my hair. She whispers, 'Keep us safe,' but I am not safe. I am not safe at all. I hear the stamp of a hoof too close, the straw scratches the bottom of my feet. If a horse were to stamp now—

'Emily.' I try to scream her name but it is just muffled syllables trapped in fabric.

'Flame, shhh. Shhh. Flame.'

Emily turns my face towards her and kisses it, kissing my cheek, my forehead, my stretched-open lips. It is a bit, and I know that I am a horse. This is a bit. She bites my cheek as I struggle away from her.

'Flame,' she says, 'come back Flame. Here boy. Here boy.' I hear her whistle. The horses stamp more fiercely.

She lifts me then onto my hands and knees. She holds my hair tight in her fist. She shifts and I feel the whole weight of her on my back, the harsh prickle of the hair between her legs as she starts to rock, forward, back, pulling my head sharply, forcing me to find the same rhythm, pushing my head down, pulling my head up. And then she is up and riding.

There is fur near my cheek, one of the horses. They are too close and they are jittery.

'Spirit of Flame, we invoke you.'

She rides. She reaches back and slaps my rump with the flat edge of her hairbrush. I don't want to play, I want to stop this now and I have no way of telling her. I groan and I dip forward, stretch back, I try to reach up, raising a hand and pulling at the gag.

'Take to the bit!' She slaps at my fingers with the brush, she tugs at my hair in her fist. I buck as hard as I can but she is strong and she can hold me if she wants to.

'Spirit of Flame we invoke you.'

And the horses. The horses are scaring me. I shake my head as hard as I can. I am sobbing and the mucus is running down my face. She slaps me harder with the brush and I can't hold us up anymore. I collapse down, my face in the straw, the hoof of a horse close to my face. Emily crouches over me. I can feel her hips rocking against mine as she rides harder, faster.

'Spirit of Flame,' she is shouting now, 'we invoke you.'

My breath is huffing out of me in sharp puffs that tear at my lungs like the desperate scrabbling of tiny birds.

I am not the first to smell the fire, and the smell of it comes before the flames. One of the patrons smells it, and the idea of the fire travels faster than the fire itself. One conversation after another silenced by the sudden troubled murmur. Then we all smell it, the whole crowd acting as one. A sudden surge towards the door.

There are people upstairs where the other artists have hung their work, the crowd is pushing at itself racing to get down and out of the building, the corners of the paintings are catching fire. One of the grey-haired men has sacrificed his suit jacket to stifle the flames on one of the paintings, but the moment he takes the coat away the canvas bursts into flames once more. I am not sure how she has orchestrated this but I can see her hand as clearly as if she has laid her cards down in front of everyone to play open misère.

Emily.

All the people are going one way and I am working my way past them in the other direction. There are too many people in this space. It is clear to me now. The space is small and the crowd is too big and somewhere in amongst it all there is Emily.

'Em?'

The hunks of horse flesh are hung on wires from the tall ceiling. Fresh meat, the blood still on it. It was easy enough before the fire to step around the horses, to stand at a little distance from the carnage, but now a horse head slaps back at me, twirling a grotesque pirouette on its wire. A Chinese woman in a pale pink dress presses past me. Her skirt is red with blood, the gore of a quartered horse.

'Emily?'

This mass panic is the installation, I see it now, pressing against the crowd I can see what she would have envisioned when she set up this work. Suits stained with blood, women in frocks trailing entrails, and Emily, master of ceremonies. Emily in her blue silk dress up on the podium. They would be facing the wrong way, this audience, but they are not the audience. There is only one audience member. The show has been played out for me alone and I am staring, as intended, at the spectacle.

I stop, holding my place in the crowd, forcing the shrieking people to push past me. Paintings on fire, the dresses, the blood, the horse meat slapping against them like macabre wind chimes, and Emily on the podium with a horse's head now fitted squarely on her shoulders, dripping blood down her blue silk dress. Fire is creeping across the hay that she has strewn on the floor, there is the back half of a horse resting on the ground in front of her, and I see the flames lick at it, the coarse fur catches, the flesh singes, the smell of it, smoke. My eyes are watering, I cough, but Emily seems unperturbed. She gallops on the spot, a childish parody of galloping. High knees jogging on the spot, hands raised like a stallion rearing, the hollowed-out shell of a horse's head dipping forward back forward back as she rides ever forward, going nowhere.

I can barely breathe. Fear takes your breath away, I know now why they say that. My chest is tight. My arms are shaking from trying to dislodge the weight of Emily on my back. The smell of the smoke is a shock. I freeze at the first whiff of it. I try to get more breath, to cry out or perhaps just to cry but my lungs are clenched with fright and now there is the smoke, thin and distant at first like thunder at a safe distance, but the smoke thickens quickly, the thunder rolls in. The storm is upon us. I struggle. The horses stamp and whinny. I hear a huge cracking sound like a beam splitting and I know that they have started to kick out. I am amongst it all, I am blind and pinned and I cough up great strings of phlegm. I want it to stop. I just want it to stop.

The roof of the gallery is high but the smoke is thick and rising. The alarm sounds, finally, and the water starts and this too is a part of the performance. A horse in the rain, dead in the rising tide, its legs kicked up towards the sky, its belly bloated. The rain falls and she gallops. The flames lick at the tops of the canvases, greedily eating the last of the portraits, singeing the wooden beams set into the walls. Fire and water. A battle.

The flames beat valiantly against the sprinklers but eventually are drowned. The blue silk clings to her body, the fabric outlines her breasts, her legs, her mane hangs limp and spent on her human shoulders, her dead horse eyes stare straight ahead unblinking. The ride is winding down, the dance is slowing, the exhibition is almost at an end. The room is empty. It is only me and Emily. It has only ever been me and Emily. I move towards her. Water drips off my chin.

The gallop slows now to a canter, a walk and then it stops completely. The performance has ended. I have to smile at her despite myself. It was beautiful. A beautiful, awful, terrifying exhibition. I stand before her and I begin to clap.

The smoke in the barn is so thick that I can barely open my eyes. The horses have bolted. I am sure of it. I can't hear their whinnying. I can't hear the crazy stamp and kick. I hold my hands in front of me like a blind girl and, like a blind girl, I look but I can't see. There is someone in here, some person who isn't Emily. Emily has fled. I see a face, so like but unlike my sister.

'Emily?' I know it is not. It is our mother here in the smoke with me. Ghostly, a frown. Awake and alert, it is our mother come to save me from my crazy sister.

My lungs ache when I run to her. My head throbs. I clutch at her arm but she shakes me off.

'Bad girl.' I have no memory of her ever speaking, the sound of her voice startles me. It is like Emily's. Here are words from my mother's mouth and it is as if one of the horses opened its mouth and began to speak.

'Do you want another baby? Do you? You'll get another baby if you carry on like that!'

Her hands slap at my naked chest, her nails tear at my skin. I fall, and there is air here, thin and acrid but I gasp at the little breath of air that finds me on the stable floor, I crawl after it, gasping.

'Barn!'

Spit flies from her mouth.

'Like an animal! In a barn! Like an animal!' and her voice cracks into a rasping cough. 'Stupid slut!' She slaps at her own face, once, and hard. And then I see the box of matches in her hand, she opens it, takes a fragile stick of wood between her fingers, lights the match and throws it. It lands beside me and I see the little glow of the straw as it catches. 'Stay away from that barn!' she spits. The same crackling noise the flame makes. I stumble on my hands and knees towards the doorway. I know it is the door because the air is suddenly rushing at me. I dive into it as if it is a stream. Voices. Emily? A man's voice. I think of Raphael but I don't know what to think about Raphael. Without Emily to tell me what to think I am rudderless. Men's voices. I run towards the sound. My eyes sting, my breath burns in my lungs. I cling to a shirt, a stranger. I am aware of my nakedness and I hunch over, dropping back to the ground.

'There's someone in there.'

I blink, look, seeing someone inside the barn.

'Emily!'

Someone is holding my arm so tight that it stings. I am pinned. I scream to her. Her name and she screams back, not my name, but a banshee calling out in the night, a spirit crossing back into the afterlife.

I see her outlined in the window, but it isn't Emily. I stare into the face of our mother. I see her, as if for the first time. The grin that I have never seen from her before, the way she opens her mouth and laughs, just like Emily, the way she raises her hands and claps. She is a woman raised from the dead, or at least woken from her drugged sleeping. Now I can see why Emily is just like her mother which is what our Oma has always said. This is my sister suddenly grown older.

'Slut!' she shouts it and this time she is laughing. The laughter turns sharp, a shriek. A wail. A sound too high and piercing to be human, the cry of an animal or a bird. Only a glimpse and then it is nothing but flame. The crack of a beam falling. The fire consuming all that is left of her.

'Emily!' I scream, staring around looking for her. But she has gone. She is nowhere to be found. Emily is gone and now I am alone.

Emily lifts the hollowed-out horse head off her shoulders and her face is smeared with red, but there is water and the blood does not last. She tucks the grotesque and bloodied thing under her arm and bows deeply. I clap and clap and eventually she stands tall on her pedestal. Her body shakes with laughter. The grin I saw on my mother's face in the window of the barn. I am back there now, I am half here and half fifteen years old. This is my sister and my mother simultaneously. A shared madness, but finally I have found my place. Witness, audience, sympathetic bystander: for once I am happy to be an observer. I do not feel left out of my sister's game.

'Fuck, Em, they'll lock you up.' I don't want to lose her again. Even when she scares me, I love my sister more than I have ever loved anyone or anything.

She laughs until the laughter changes and then she is crying.

I move to touch her arm. 'It was a good exhibition. The paintings, even the meat. It was a good exhibition. You didn't need to set the place on fire.'

Emily steps off the pedestal. 'Raphael—'

'Raphael? Emily. Come on.'

Emily slumps onto the rostrum and holds her palms up and flat to catch the rain from the fire extinguishers. 'Raphael must have burned the barn down, Bec. I didn't. I swear.'

'I know you didn't. Mother did it, I saw her.'

She is confused. She narrows her eyes. 'But you never came to see me.'

'They kept me away.' It is true, but it is not an excuse. I could have tracked her down. I could have found her.

'Well.' She shrugs then, a little gesture of resignation. 'I started this one.'

She splashes water on her face and grins. 'It was good though, wasn't it? The paintings? The fire? The rain? And no one died this time. Did you notice that? I did it so no one died.'

'Yeah,' I tell her, 'it was good. It was great, actually. I've never seen anything like it.'

'Raphael wanted to do it for your birthday.'

I feel my chest sink like a balloon deflating.

'They'll put you back in hospital.'

'Yeah,' she says. 'But don't you think it's time I went back now anyway?'

Kite

The plan is to get the thing in the air before he notices. The winds are erratic. I have never been to his apartment and now I know why he always preferred to come to mine. The place is an ugly brick monolith. Washing hangs from some of the balconies, a boogie board leans up against a wall. The outdoor furniture on each level is cheap plastic. Someone has thrown an egg from somewhere and the shattered fragments of shell sit, a crusted yellow stucco at my feet. There is a ragged Australian flag hung in a doorway. Someone else has blocked the light with a curtain branded with Bob Marley's face. There is the scent of tobacco and just a hint of pot wafting from the open windows.

An erratic breeze tugs at the kite and sends it diving into the ground where its nose cracks on the hot bitumen. I aim the crossbar into another gust, pull at the string. The kite almost finds the current, teeters, loops. A change in wind direction sends it clattering into someone's standing candelabra and I grab the string in my fist and haul but it is too late.

'Hey.'

I am often surprised by him. He is always more attractive in the flesh than in memory. I think it must be something in his face, the gentle eyes, the softness around the mouth; anyway, I am startled by the power of my attraction to him.

'That's blown it,' I tell him and his brow furrows, questioning. 'The plan was to get that thing in the air then call you.' I hold out my mobile phone. His name hovers on the screen with a photograph of him beneath it.

'Oh. That was a good idea. Would you like me to go back inside?'

'Don't bother. It's too late now. It wouldn't be a surprise anymore.'

'No. And also I don't think we have the appropriate weather conditions for the plan to succeed completely.'

'Yeah.'

'But I suppose that's my present from China?'

I hold out my hand. He takes the string and tries to reel it in. The kite stops flat against the railing and will not budge. He jumps, twitching the line upward, but it refuses to move.

'It looks like a nice kite anyway.'

He jumps again and plays the line left and then right but it is stuck fast.

'Damn,' he says. 'That guy who lives there is pretty scary. He plays in a death metal band called Backslasher. Sometimes the rest of the band come round and turn their guitars up really loud and throw their empties at the cars on the street.'

'Awesome.'

'Totally.' He puts his hand out as if to touch my shoulder and thinks better of it, crossing his hands awkwardly over his chest instead.

'How are you?'

'Not as bad as you'd think. Which is odd actually.'

'Yeah, sorry to hear about your sister.'

'She'll be okay.'

'But the way the news reported it made it sound like a fantastic exhibition. Everyone is jealous of you for being there to see it.'

His hand moves forward again just a little and I step into the familiar embrace. The smell of him, the sheer physicality. 'It was. It was fantastic.' I close my eyes and pause there for a moment before stepping away. 'Anyway we probably have to get the kite back from the drummer.'

'Bass player. Yeah. I'll go up and ask him in a bit.'

'Cause there's an envelope stuck onto it.'

'Oh yeah? What's in it? A lottery ticket?'

I laugh.

'Some Chinese money? That was great that Chinese money you sent me with Mao's face on it and everything.'

'It's a ticket. To a thing at the Gallery of Modern Art.'

'Oh cool. Everyone is all over your sister again now. I knew they would want to do something.'

'Not exactly. It's my thing. They want to do something on me. A solo exhibition.'

He lunges at me and hugs me and lifts me up so that my feet are dangling above the ground. He jigs me like a doll, up and down in his arms and I am laughing with him. When he puts me back on the ground his cheeks are flushed with his excitement and something else.

Pride. John is proud, I realise suddenly, surprisingly. John is proud of me.

'You better get painting then.'

'Oh god no. I have plenty of paintings. I just had to get them out of storage.'

He grins at me and I like him, a lot. I like him an awful lot.

'Oi!' he yells up towards the balcony, a deep rich sound echoing off the flat brick of the apartment block. 'Backslasher dude. Come the fuck outside, I need to get my fucking kite!'

Signature Works

Lined up like this they take up the wall space along the entire room. The studio is the length and breadth of the house and even with the edges of the canvases pressed close against each other there are still seven paintings resting face up on the centre of the floor. They are somehow naked without a signature. I have managed to match the paint almost perfectly. You can barely see where my sister's name has been removed. Each painting has a person staring directly at me, their eyes a challenge. They watch me as I pace around the makeshift gallery.

Original Emily Reichs, and yet when I see them like this, without her faked signature, I know that they are not like Emily's paintings at all. They are similar in subject, people become animals, animals begin to burn. But they have my own touch on them, ambiguous smiles, an enigmatic emotional shift that you can't quite pin down.

John smiles up out of one of the canvases, his lips slightly parted as if he is just about to speak. It is impossible to know if what he is about to say is funny, sad or poignant, all I have captured on this canvas is the sweet, kind face of a man about to speak.

I choose a thin brush, but not the slimmest of them, full enough to give substance to the line I am about to make. It is odd to sign the image with my own name, but when it is done it feels like it was the right thing to do.

Bec Reich. This is a painting by me now. All of these, more than enough to fill a gallery space twice over. I move on from the painting of John to the next painting and the next, putting my name to images of my students, the staff at work, my psychiatrist, the nurses at Oma's hospital, the lady at the shop where I buy bread. These faces captured between thoughts, between moods, in a state of transition, all of them shifted now from paintings by my sister to images that I have claimed.

My wrist aches. There are so many repetitions of my signature to perform. My back hurts from bending and I stretch out and up, twist my wrist till it clicks. My name repeated back to me a hundred times. Bec Reich. I am Bec Reich and these paintings are made by me.

Thank-yous

I gratefully acknowledge the support of Varuna Writers' House for the completion of this book.

Thanks to my editor Mandy Brett and to all at Text. You are the best publishing house bar none.

To my first readers, Katherine Lyall-Watson, Chris Somerville, Trent Jamieson, Favel Parrett, Martin Cosier, Kristina Olsson, Anna Goldsworthy and my reader and love Anthony Mullins. Thank you to Fiona Stager for the constant emotional and career support. To Chris Currie for company during the writing of the first draft of this and for minding my computer when nature called. To Jen Clark, Martin Cosier, Sally Brand and Carl Flanagan for China. To Bouquinest Café for letting me use your table as an office.

Thanks to my family, Barry and Denise, Wendy, Lotty and Sheila and of course my sister, Karen. This book is not about you but I love you.

To my writing and reading family, Benjamin Law, Scott Spark, Belinda Jeffrey, Kari Gislason, Kristina Schulz, Ronnie Scott, James Butler, Kasia Janczewski, Jason Reed, Helen Bernhagen, Michaela Maguire, Anna Krien, Angela Meyer, Anita Heiss, Steven Amsterdam, Michelle Law, Simon Cleary, Stuart Glover, Susan Hornbeck, Jack Vening, Ashley Hay, John Hunter, Marieke Hardy, Matt Condon, Steve Watson, Nicholas Ib, the Cosier family and Jay Court—thanks for the comforting texts, coffees, alcohol, jokes and messages of support during the good and awful bits.

Lastly thanks to all those involved in the 2012 Queensland Literary Awards. I am so proud of what we did and I am sorry that this book distracted me from the last few weeks of our mammoth effort. Hope you think it was worth it.